[illegible] a journalist, a travel courier, a [illegible]onist and a history teacher. After turning to full-time [illegible]ng, Hebden created a sequence of crime novels, [illegible]ting the well-known character of Inspector Pel.

BY THE SAME AUTHOR
ALL PUBLISHED BY HOUSE OF STRATUS

THE DARK SIDE OF THE ISLAND
DEATH SET TO MUSIC
THE ERRANT KNIGHTS
EYE WITNESS
A KILLER FOR THE CHAIRMAN
LEAGUE OF EIGHTY NINE
MASK OF VIOLENCE
PEL AMONG THE PUEBLOS
PEL AND THE TOUCH OF PITCH
PEL AND THE BOMBERS
PEL AND THE FACELESS CORPSE
PEL AND THE MISSING PERSONS
PEL AND THE PARIS MOB
PEL AND THE PARTY SPIRIT
PEL AND THE PICTURE OF INNOCENCE
PEL AND THE PIRATES
PEL AND THE PROMISED LAND
PEL AND THE PROWLER
PEL AND THE SEPULCHRE JOB
PEL AND THE STAG HOUND
PEL IS PUZZLED
PEL UNDER PRESSURE
PORTRAIT IN A DUSTY FRAME
A PRIDE OF DOLPHINS
WHAT CHANGED CHARLEY FARTHING

Pel and the Predators

MARK HEBDEN

This edition published in 2001 by House of Stratus, an imprint of Stratus Holdings plc, 24c Old Burlington Street, London, W1X 1RL, UK.

www.houseofstratus.com

Typeset, printed and bound by House of Stratus.

A catalogue record for this book is available from the British Library.

ISBN 1-84232-897-2

Though Burgundians will probably decide they have recognised it – and certainly many of its street names are the same – in fact the city in these pages is intended to be fictitious.

one

The early morning sun was brilliant but there was a strong wind that flung the waves ashore like the regiments of an attacking army.

The old man moving along the beach barely noticed. He had his head down and was collecting driftwood. During the summer he collected sufficient to keep his fire alight throughout the winter and, with coal as costly as diamonds, it was quite an achievement. He pulled a plank out of the water to a point where the rising tide couldn't reach it, intending to collect it later with a barrow he'd made from the frame of an old perambulator, and fished out a rope attached to two bright blue plastic balls. In his day nets had been supported by cork floats which you cut yourself. Nowadays everything was manufactured – probably inland, too, he thought with a sniff by people who knew nothing about the sea.

The little pile of timber grew and he was just about to call it a day when he noticed what looked like a red rubber sphere, bobbing among the rocks. It was probably a pill buoy, he decided, and he might get something for it from one of the fishermen – even if only a drink. Trudging down the beach, his yellow rubber boots leaving long slurred footprints, he moved along the water's edge, deciding his walk had been for nothing and that the red object was nothing more than a punctured airbed. Then he realised it was a plastic rubber raincoat, the sort he'd seen holidaymakers wear on the days when the Breton coast lived up to its reputation and brought gales and rain. Then he stopped dead because he could now also see a pale greyish-looking hand, slashed with wet sand and entwined with a coil of dark green seaweed, protruding from the sleeve and resting across a small rock.

Nervously, he moved closer. He had dragged many dead people from the sea in his time and bodies were nothing to upset him. But now that he was old, he didn't enjoy finding them because they made him realise how short was his own life span. He crept closer and, peering over the rocks, saw long hair moving in the swirls of water. It was a young woman, he could see now, and he turned abruptly and began to shuffle up the beach to where he had left his bicycle.

He was out of breath when he reached the police station. As he stumbled through the door, he was able only to gasp out his message a few words at a time.

'I've found a girl...'

The policeman behind the counter looked up. He was young, bright, breezy and full of the joy of life. 'You're lucky,' he said, regarding the old man with the contemptuous pity of the young for the ageing. 'I've just lost mine. Chucked me for a fisherman.'

'No...no...' Struggling for breath, the old man waved his arms. 'I've found this girl...'

'At your age, too!'

The old man glared at the policeman, stood silently for a second or two, then very deliberately turned away and, watched by the policeman, sat down on a polished seat opposite the counter, his eyes glowing with hatred. Gradually his chest stopped heaving and he rose slowly to his feet. Crossing back to the policeman, he stood at the counter and drew a deep breath.

'I've found a girl,' he said slowly and carefully so there should be no misunderstanding. 'On the beach.'

The young policeman couldn't resist it. 'Topless?' he asked.

It was too much for the old man. He snatched off his cap and flung it at the policeman, then he slammed his ancient fists down on the counter top and bellowed with all the power in his lungs.

'I've found a girl on the beach!' he roared. 'And, if you'd only listen for a minute, you stupid young con, you'd understand that I'm trying to say she's dead!'

In Burgundy, spring had come early and the enamelled roofs for which the city was famous glowed in the golden light of the warm sunshine. Though it was an up-to-date thriving city packed with pedestrians and traffic, there were always odd corners which belonged to the Middle Ages, so that the solemn buildings, old courtyards and dim alleys seemed in the dusk as if they ought to be peopled in the bizarre splendour of the Valois court, with women in wimples and trailing dresses and men with swords and striped hose. It was often referred to as 'the city of a hundred belfries' but so was Rouen and doubtless a dozen other places too, and Evariste Clovis Désiré Pel of the Brigade Criminelle of the Police Judiciaire wasn't one to dwell much on fantasies. A Burgundian to his finger tips, he was as proud of his city as he was of the rolling land that surrounded it, land that produced fat cattle, rich grain and the finest wine in France. When the wine of Bordeaux was mentioned, Pel usually looked blank and asked 'What's that?' though he had recently begun to notice that, for a late evening meal, Burgundy sat somewhat heavily on the stomach while the lighter wine of Bordeaux gave no trouble. As a good Burgundian, it seemed blasphemy to admit it but one had to face the facts of advancing age.

At the moment, however, his heart was light and that was a change because with Evariste Clovis Désiré Pel it often wasn't. A policeman's life, he felt was too real and too earnest for such frivolities as light hearts and, in addition, he suffered from insomnia, overwork, shortage of money, and the unquestionable, indubitable fact that he smoked too much. In recent months he'd cut his cigarettes down from two million a day to around five hundred thousand but he was well aware that it still wasn't half enough and the effort to do better left him edgy with nerves.

Today, though, was different. He had just been informed that he had been promoted to chief inspector and that his job had changed. For some time now, in addition to his normal duties, he had been investigating complaints and checking police stations and substations for inefficiency, but it had finally occurred to the authorities that they were wasting their best detective in a job that was within the powers of a mere organisation man, and the Chief had informed him that morning that he was back at his old job, the job he liked best – striking terror into the hearts of the criminals who threatened to undermine the structure of the French Republic. Pel's attitude to crime was a crusader's attitude – uncomplicated and intense.

The Chief had given a little party to celebrate the promotion. One or two senior legal names were there: Judge Polverari, for one, who was a friend of Pel's and liked to take him out for expensive meals just for the pleasure of hearing his astringent comments on other people – Judge Brisard, for instance, whom Pel liked in the way you liked amputations. The Maire, who was elected by the people to do what they wanted, and the Prefect, who was set over him by Central Government to stop him, were also present, with the Public Prosecutor, his deputy and his clerk, and a few heads of local government departments. The gathering was held in an echoing room off the council chamber, with a bust representing the Republic on the mantelpiece, a tricolour, and a pile of books on social security on a polished table. The carpet was green and so expansive it felt as if they were holding a party in the middle of a football field.

The Chief made the position clear. 'Goriot's decided he won't be up to the job when he comes out of hospital – ' Inspector Goriot, Pel's nearest rival, had recently been wounded in an affray in the city which had made the storming of the Bastille look like a Sunday afternoon outing ' – so we're giving him your job of co-ordinator. You'll take over his team as well as your own and run two groups.'

Pel nodded. No matter what anybody else intended, he intended to continue as before, as he always had – as the Nemesis of the criminal classes – the only difference being that for a change he would now have enough help.

'You'd better inform your men,' the Chief said. 'It's going to cost you something in drinks, I imagine, when they know.'

There was always a fly in the ointment, no matter how splendid the treatment. And first, anyway, there was one before even his men whom Pel had to inform. Deep down, despite his frozen face, he was more pleased that he would ever admit. Promotion meant a bigger office, a higher salary and better expenses, all of which was something to crow about, and he hoped it would impress.

The affair between Pel and Madame Geneviève Faivre-Perret had been going on some time now, long enough in fact for the Hôtel de Police to start hoping for a successful conclusion, if only to improve Pel's temper. There had been interruptions from time to time, of course, such as were caused by Madame's relatives, who had an unfortunate habit of dying every time Pel made a date, or by the exigencies of his job, because every time he got Madame on her own somebody seemed to get beaten up, raped, assaulted, or even murdered, and Pel had never been certain, anyway, that he could afford marriage. Now, at long last – despite the fact that like a squirrel with nuts he'd been stuffing money into the bank for years against a poverty-stricken old age, he was finally beginning to feel marriage wouldn't bankrupt him.

He met Madame at the Hôtel Central for an apéritif that evening. The Central was the best hotel in the city and the manager appeared to greet them. He knew Pel well but he knew Madame Faivre-Perret better. Madame was a business woman who attended business meetings in the hotel and sometimes ate business lunches there because she owned Nanette's, the largest and most fashionable hairdressing establishment in the city, a place where they didn't have charges, they had fees. Pel was merely a policeman and, though the hotel had had cause to be grateful to the police from time to time over the activities of certain of its guests who were not all they pretended to be, the manager wasn't all that keen on policemen making free with his hotel as customers. Having them, even in plain clothes, sitting there drinking could get the place a bad name.

Madame Faivre-Perret listened to Pel's news with amusement dancing in her eyes. By this time she knew Pel well.

'Evariste – ' she was a widow and, having to look after herself, was not in the habit of beating about the bush ' – are you asking me to marry you?'

Pel looked blank. 'I thought I did,' he said. 'Some time ago.'

'No, Evariste. Never. Perhaps you assumed. *I* never have.'

'Then – ' Pel swallowed, nervously aware of the abyss into which he was stepping ' – then – will you?'

'I've been wondering when you were going to get around to it.' She looked at him worriedly. 'You do want to, don't you?'

Pel could hardly speak for the earnestness of his reply. He looked forward to marriage as one condemned to death looked forward to the man on the white horse hurtling up with the reprieve tucked into his gauntlet. For years he had lived with the indifferent ministrations of Madame Routy, his housekeeper, who was probably the only bad cook in a country crammed full of culinary experts. She stole the 'confort anglais,' the only comfortable chair in his house, gossiped with the neighbours and suffered from an addiction to television which took the form of watching everything from breakfast time to the good night kiss, always with the volume turned up beyond 'Loud' to 'Unbelievable.' He had been convinced for a long time that the deplorable state of his house was entirely due to the stresses and strains placed on the foundations by the vibrations set up by the shuddering one-eyed box in his salon.

'Of course,' he said fervently. 'It's my dearest wish.'

Madame smiled, reassured, and put on her spectacles to see him better. She was a little on the short-sighted side which, Pel often considered, was probably a good thing for him because he was not a very prepossessing man and, with his thin hair plastered across his skull like wet seaweed across a rock, he sometimes felt he looked a little like an anxious terrier.

On the other hand, of course, if she could choose someone as unimpressive as himself – and one also with the Christian names Evariste Clovis Désiré – she *had* to feel something for him. His mother had hoped his future might be in politics – and certainly Evariste Clovis Désiré seemed to go more with a president of France than a chief inspector of the Police Judiciaire – but she could never have conceived the way the names she'd chosen weighed at times on her son.

'It's so easy, really,' Madame Faivre-Perret was saying. 'I have a business which is doing splendidly. You've been promoted to a position of importance. There's nothing to stop us.'

Pel sat back in his seat. Now the thing was done, he was caught by a cold fear. After a lifetime of independence, had he thrown it all up in the name of company, comfort and decent food? He drew a deep breath. It seemed to call for another drink.

As the drinks arrived, Madame got down to arrangements.

'I shall give up my house at Talant, of course,' she said.

Pel looked alarmed. Surely she wasn't thinking of moving into the house he maintained in the Rue Martin-de-Noinville? His house looked like a dilapidated chicken run and, because he was a little on the mean side, hadn't been decorated for years so that it seemed – even to Pel – to have been curtained with sacking and papered with wrapping paper.

'We shall need something larger,' Madame said placidly.

'Shall we?' Pel was wondering what his impulsiveness had led him to. Marriage suddenly seemed a very expensive business. The thought made him feel in need of a cigarette but he resisted the temptation. Now that he was acquiring a wife, he felt, he couldn't possibly afford both.

'Actually,' he said, 'we shall need a new car, too. I've been expecting mine to let me down for years.'

Madame laughed. '*I*'ve been expecting it to deposit me in the gutter every time we go round a corner.' She touched Pel's hand. 'I think perhaps we'll be able to afford both. I'm not without funds.'

Relief flooded over Pel. 'I was thinking of a bungalow at Plombières,' he suggested. His mind had been full for some time of a neat little property in the country, near the river where he could fish, perhaps with a garden that could be made – by someone else, of course, he decided firmly – to produce vegetables which would offset the enormous expense of supporting a wife. Perhaps even a dog, so he could walk out in the evening, a countryman looking round his estate. He decided against a stick and a pipe in the English manner. The last time he'd tried a pipe to stop himself smoking cigarettes he had ended up with jaw ache, a sour mouth and a burned hole in his pocket.

'I was thinking of something at Hauteville just north of Fontaine,' Madame said.

'That's a very expensive area.' Like a recalcitrant underslip, Pel's alarm was beginning to show again.

She was quite unperturbed. 'There are a few people about the city who can find me something. Businessmen I know.'

Pel's heart shrivelled with jealousy at the thought of other men sharing Madame with him.

'A garden, perhaps,' she went on. 'Fields, so we don't feel too enclosed. An orchard. Two bathrooms. A big salon.'

Name of God, Pel thought in a panic, it was growing bigger by the minute! It was already the size of a château and the costs would bankrupt him.

She noticed his look and began to tease a little. 'You'll need a study, too, of course. Somewhere you can read all those documents you have to go through.'

Pel looked shocked. 'I will?'

'And I think if we're to live at Hauteville I shall need transport into the city when you're busy. We'll need two cars.'

Holy Mother of God, Pel thought, what had he taken on?

Her next words made him sag with relief.

'Of course, I wouldn't expect you to provide all this. I have the house at Vitteaux that my aunt left me when she died. I thought we'd sell it and buy something on a lake. Perhaps in the Jura. Somewhere to go at weekends. So you can relax.'

Pel was all for having a house by a lake in the Jura, but he couldn't see himself relaxing much. Relaxing didn't come easily to Pel and he called in at the Hôtel de Police every evening to check up on things even when he wasn't on duty, just in case the place fell down, or somebody – someone who wasn't a Burgundian and unfortunately there were many such who'd been allowed to sneak across the border into the province – wasn't paying proper attention to his job.

He was just basking in pleasant thoughts of a secure old age when he saw Darcy appear in the hotel lounge with a girl. Inspector Daniel Darcy was his second-in-command, a handsome young man with a ready smile he liked to use a lot so that his teeth showed to good advantage. Like his girls, Darcy's teeth were too perfect, too numerous and almost too good to be true.

'Hello, Patron,' he said. 'Celebrating your promotion?'

Pel mumbled something, never very willing to share Madame Faivre-Perret with anyone else, especially Darcy, who had too much of a way with women – and not just young women either.

'It ought to be champagne,' Darcy said and turned to click his fingers at the waiter. No uncertain gesture like Pel's, but a peremptory summons which the waiter was quick to acknowledge.

'Champagne,' Darcy ordered and, without so much as a by-your-leave, with nothing more than the briefest of introductions, he and his girl friend sat down. Despite Pel's sulky looks, Madame seemed quite happy to make it a party and in no time, to Pel's envious fury, she was laughing at some joke Darcy was telling her so that Pel began to feel that if he didn't interrupt soon Darcy would be usurping his place. While Pel had spent too little of his life in other people's beds, Darcy had probably spent too much and was just a little too experienced.

He cleared his throat and his voice came out almost too loud. 'Just come from the office?'

Darcy turned his head, surprised at the interruption. 'Yes, Patron.'

'Anything happening?'

'Nothing much.'

'You mean there *is* something happening.'

'Nothing to worry us.' Darcy's attitude to police work was different from Pel's; he was inclined to regard it only as a necessary evil best ignored until it arrived in his lap. 'Just a bit of fuss from the police at Concarneau.'

'Concarneau? In Brittany? What have we to do with Concarneau?'

'They fished a girl out of the sea at Beg Meil and they think she came from round here. Suicide, they thought. It's nothing of importance. Nothing to cause *us* any work.'

Though Darcy didn't know it, he couldn't have been more wrong.

The following morning when Pel arrived in his office, Darcy appeared with a file in his hand. Philippe Duche's escaped,' he said.

'Duche?'

'We pulled him in for that job at Zamenhofs'. Him and his mob. His mother died and he was let out for the funeral and some silly con took his eye off him for a couple of seconds so that he nipped through a window. Uniformed Branch's got a full-scale search on for him.'

'They ought to find him.'

'They ought to, but they might not. He knows the city.'

'Are we involved?'

'*You* are, Patron. He's sworn to get you.' Darcy opened the file and glanced inside. 'The prison governor's let us know. While he was safely under lock and key it didn't seem to matter. Now he's out, it does.'

Pel shrugged. 'Well,' he said. 'We'll worry about that when it happens. More than likely, he'll bolt south, join one of the Marseilles gangs, and live in luxury for the rest of his life on the proceeds, with a Mercedes, a villa at St. Trop' and a mistress of unsurpassing beauty. I'm not worried and we have things to do. We need to organise the new set-up.'

He pulled a list forward. 'Yourself,' he said, reading off names as Darcy drew up a chair, 'Nosjean, De Troquereau, Lagé, Misset. The old team. Together with Aimedieu, Brochard and Debray from Goriot's team, and Lacocq and Morell from Uniformed Branch, with Claudie Darel to look after the feminine angle and Cadet Martin to take care of the office.'

'I thought they wanted *two* teams, Patron.'

'I don't think much of this Grand Quartier Général stuff,' Pel said cheerfully. 'There will be *one* team, with me at the head of it, you as deputy, and Nosjean as senior sergeant. However, for the benefit of the authorities we'll have two lists and two organisations, all on paper and very clearly defined so we'll know exactly how to ignore it.'

Darcy grinned and Pel smiled back at him. 'Better have Nosjean in and let him know.'

Nosjean blushed as they informed him what was to happen. He was still young but he had ideas and, like Darcy, was never behind the door when it came to work. At the moment he was particularly preoccupied with his job because, to his astonishment and disgust, his girl friend had unexpectedly married a man who worked in the tax office and he was still working twice as hard as normal to avoid rushing off to join the Foreign Legion.

'Right, mon brave,' Pel said briskly as he rose. 'You can run things from tomorrow. There's another break-in at the supermarket at Talant. That place has intruders like most people have mice. A wounding at Noray, that death at Marvillers – it's probably suicide but we have to make sure – the assault at Germaine, those ducks missing from Boyer's farm at Cholley – there's a history of a feud with a farmer next door called Jeanneny and Boyer's a friend of the Chief's so you'd better get on with it – that theft of petrol from the garage at Loublanc and these people who're terrorising the Montchapet district.'

After that, Nosjean thought sarcastically, you can go home and have breakfast before coming in to pick up the list for the rest of the day.

'What about Inspector Darcy?' he asked.

Pel looked up. He and Darcy had arranged to have lunch together to celebrate Pel's promotion.

'He has a lot on,' he said, a trifle stiffly. 'This body they found at Beg Meil.'

Nosjean had heard of the dead girl at Beg Meil because requests for information had already arrived in the Hôtel de Police. It didn't sound the sort of thing, he thought bitterly, that could keep Darcy very heavily involved for long.

As it happened, Nosjean was wrong, too.

two

When Pel and Darcy returned from their lunch, both of them feeling very mellow, Régis Martin, the cadet who looked after the mail, answered the telephone and brought in the bottles of beer from the Bar Transvaal across the road when the weather was hot, put his head round the door. 'The Chief wants you, Patron,' he said.

The Chief was reading reports with his feet on the desk and he was surprised when Pel refused the brandy he offered. It wasn't a habit of Pel's to refuse drinks.

'Been celebrating your promotion?' he asked.

Pel frowned. He'd been hoping it didn't show. 'Lunch with Darcy,' he said. 'To get things sorted out.'

'Right.' The Chief tossed a file across. 'Concarneau wants someone to go over there. This body they took out of the sea at Beg Meil.'

'I thought it was a suicide. Some kid on drugs.'

'They're having second thoughts. I'd like you to go.' The Chief gestured. 'Good will for one thing. This co-operation nonsense they're so keen on in Paris. And I want you to represent us at the funeral of Commissaire Habec at Rennes. He was a big man in his day. Somebody's got to go, and as I've got that enquiry at Lyons it has to be you. You can go on to Concarneau the following day. I've telephoned the Chief there. He's an old friend of mine and he'll probably meet you himself.' He gave Pel a beaming smile that was supposed to reduce all his objections to nothing. It didn't, of course.

'Concarneau's about as far as you can get from here without falling in the sea,' Pel said bitterly. Concarneau was not only outside Burgundy – and to Pel anything beyond the frontiers of his native province was a wilderness – it was almost outside France, beyond which, to Pel, a Frenchman if ever there was one, there was only darkness. Besides, he thought fretfully, he'd been hoping to spend the evening with Madame discussing once more their plans for the future. He hadn't realised just how well off she was and making plans that involved spending a lot of money appealed to him.

Madame was disappointed that she wouldn't be seeing him for a day or two, but she was beginning to get used to the demands of his job.

'I'll have to get someone responsible to run the business for me,' she said. 'Then I'll be able to come with you. Make it a holiday.'

Pel didn't fancy her chances. Police enquiries didn't normally end up as holidays. They were invariably boring and long-drawn-out and he couldn't really imagine her sitting alone in strange resting places while he did his round of police stations.

He spent the night at Rennes in an uncomfortable hotel near the station. Feeling it was necessary to hoard every penny now that they had finally decided on marriage, he looked for somewhere cheap and rather overdid it. The bed was hard and the food tasted as if it had been prepared by Madame Routy, and he bolted for the station the following morning as if the hounds of hell were after him. And when he stepped off the train at his destination, it wasn't the Chief who met him, but a detective inspector called Le Bihan. He was enormously fat, so fat that no matter where Pel stood he seemed to be there, too. However, he had his perspectives right.

'Lunch first,' he said. 'I've fixed you a hotel. When you've cleaned up we'll eat.'

There were enough apéritifs to make Pel want to fall asleep with his head in the hors d'oeuvre and the meal was an enormous repast at a splendid restaurant where Le Bihan seemed to be a favourite customer.

'My cousin runs it,' he explained.

He was smiling as he took Pel back to his office where he sat him down in a chair and began to produce photographs. They didn't reveal the dead woman but what she'd become, sad and bedraggled despite the attempts to clean her up.

'When was she found?' Pel asked.

'Twenty-third of the month. She's a mess, isn't she? The doctor decided she'd been in the sea about a week. That means she went in about the 16th. Want to see her?'

Pal wondered what he was getting at. 'Do I need to?'

'Thought you might like to.'

'Why might I like to?'

Le Bihan ignored the question. 'She was found near the rocks. She could have gone in anywhere to the west because the tide sets along the coast from that direction. We put her down as being in her late twenties. No indication of what she was, but she's not much muscled so if she worked at all she did a sedentary job. Clerk. Typist. Something like that. Hair thick and mousy-blonde. Eyes blue. Probably had a good figure and wasn't bad-looking. Wearing the usual clothing.' Le Bihan pushed over a list. 'It's all there. She'd lost her shoes but otherwise she was fully dressed, even including a light plastic raincoat. We've checked everything for laundry marks but there's nothing. The stuff was all inexpensive so she probably did her own washing. Identifying marks: A scar along her eyebrow. Probably done as a child. The usual vaccination marks. We've fingerprinted her but that's no help unless she's got a record and she doesn't seem to have; we've also checked her teeth and put out a request for dentists to look at their records. Unfortunately, since it takes time, they don't always bother. After all, who cares? If she's not your wife or your sister or your child, does it matter?'

'You're a philosopher.'

'I'm a cop,' Le Bihan said. 'I'd like to identify her but the photographs we took would be no good. She was in the water too long. However, there are one or two things that might help.' He pushed forward a photograph which had been taken of the inside of the girl's elbow. Despite a certain amount of decomposition, marks clearly showed on the soft flesh of the joint. 'She'd been on drugs, even if she wasn't on them when she died. Got anybody like that missing in your area?'

Pel was still wondering why so much importance was being attached to the case, why, in fact, he'd been dragged all the way across France. Suicides didn't normally merit such interest.

'Should I have?' he asked.

'Well, she comes from your area.' Le Bihan opened a brown envelope and spread its contents on the table. 'Labels show that for the most part she bought her clothes in Paris supermarkets. No identification papers or driving licence but a twenty-franc note and six centimes in her pocket. Handkerchief. Make-up compact.' The articles slid along the table one after the other. 'Lipstick. Comb. Eyeliner. Handkerchief. Piece of paper bearing the words, "8 p.m. Bar Giorgiou." Got a Bar Giorgiou in your area?'

'My area's roughly the size of Brittany,' Pel pointed out coldly.

'Looks as if she made an appointment,' Le Bihan went on. 'And it led to her death.'

'Unless she'd arranged to meet her mother to go shopping.'

Le Bihan looked up sharply. He wasn't used to Pel's sense of humour. 'Finally,' he said. 'This.'

'This' was a photograph of a label.

'Found on her dress,' Le Bihan said. 'A dress that was the exception to all her other garments in that it was expensive.' His finger rested on the photograph and Pel caught the name. 'Mirabelle, Dijon.'

'Your area,' Le Bihan said. 'We telephoned them, of course, and I gather this is a line they've been carrying only this year, so it was bought fairly recently. They looked up their records of cheques but there was nothing to indicate who our little friend was, so we have to assume the dress was paid for in cash. And that raises another question: what would a woman her age be doing with a handbag full of cash to pay for a dress like this when she had only twenty francs on her when we pulled her from the sea? It doesn't make sense. And why was she wearing an expensive dress but cheap underwear and a cheap plastic raincoat? Is she a skivvy who helped herself to one of her employer's garments? Was she given the dress? If so, by whom? Is she some shop assistant who helped herself from the shelves and went on a spree? Is she a millionaire's daughter who was trying to pass incognito – some wealthy young philanthropist who wanted to see how the other half lived? Or is she just another foreign spy in Brittany to watch the naval base at St. Nazaire?'

'You should try writing novels,' Pel said dryly.

Le Bihan smiled. 'I've often thought it might be a good job,' he admitted. 'Just sitting with your feet on the desk with a notepad and a ball-point.'

'I imagine there's more to it than that.'

'I guess so.' Le Bihan grinned.

'And one label on a dress doesn't mean she comes from our area.'

'I suspect she does, all the same. Because of this.' Le Bihan produced a small square of pulpy lavender paper, on which were printed the words 'Cavernes de Coron, 3 fr. 50.'

'It's an entrance ticket,' he said. 'To a set of caves. I looked them up. They admit the public. They're at Drax which again is in your area.'

'I've heard of them,' Pel agreed.

'Discovered by lead miners eighty years ago. On a farm owned by a type called Coron. It came from her pocket so she'd obviously been there. The ticket number, according to Coron, indicates it was Ascension Day, when they were open for the holiday. Why?'

Pel was unmoved. 'You tell me,' he said.

Le Bihan pulled from his pocket a pipe that looked as if it had been carved from a tree trunk, knotty, shapeless and ugly, and began to stuff it with tobacco. Then, carefully, as if he regarded it as almost too delicate for his large hands, he produced a gold chain with, in its centre, a small chased gold heart. It was incredibly fine and seemed to call for all the delicacy of touch Le Bihan was showing. He turned the heart decoration over and handed Pel a magnifying glass. In the centre of the back was a single minute word, 'Lucie.'

'Got any shapely young females in your area called "Lucie" who can afford to pay cash down for expensive dresses at Mirabelle's?' he asked. 'Though it's our case, it looks as if the lady belongs to you.'

Pel was still puzzled. 'Do you usually go to all this trouble for a suicide?' he asked.

'Ah!' Le Bihan smiled. 'That's the point, you see. At first I decided she'd been drowned. Walked into the sea. Depression. Frustration. That sort of thing. Perhaps unemployed. Boy friend trouble. Flung out of home. Nowhere to go.'

'You *should* try writing novels,' Pel said. 'You could be good at it.'

Le Bihan shrugged. 'Just using my imagination, that's all. She was in the sea with syringe marks on her arm. Drugs. Depression. They go together. I was just working out a line.

Only – ' he smiled again ' – only she *wasn't* drowned.' He tossed across several sheets of typed paper stapled together. 'Pathologist's report. It was the absence of blood that made us think of drowning, but, of course, the blood had all been washed away by the sea. Besides, she had a lot of thick hair that covered the abrasions and wounds and she *looked* drowned. But when the pathologist got down to it he found she hadn't drowned. She had a fractured skull.'

'Go on,' Pel said, beginning to grow interested. 'Inform me.'

Le Bihan seemed pleased that he'd finally roused him. He sucked at his unlit pipe thoughtfully. It sounded like a bus reversing. 'The post mortem,' he said, 'showed there was no water in her lungs. And, as you know as well as I do, I'm sure, that indicates she wasn't alive when she was put in the sea. The pathologist also discovered the remains of heavy bruising along her back, buttocks, legs and chest. Also a fractured pelvis, and several crushed ribs. What does that indicate to you?'

'Motor car?'

'That's my view. It was also the pathologist's view. So it then began to look like a hit-and-run. I now saw her depressed, lonely, wandering about in the dark. Perhaps she'd been drinking and was unaware of the approaching traffic.'

'Let's just say,' Pel suggested mildly, 'that she was knocked down. Without the trimmings. And that whoever did it panicked and put her in the sea, hoping you'd assume it was suicide.'

Le Bihan grinned. 'All right. No dramatics. That's exactly what I thought. All the same, an unreported accident's against the law and a hit-and-run killing can be manslaughter.'

'There's one other thing, too,' Pet said. 'Was she pregnant?'

'Ah,' Le Bihan said. 'That occurred to me, too. Yes, she was. Three months.'

'In which case,' Pel pointed out, 'it might even be murder.'

'Exactly.'

There was a long silence while Pel looked at Le Bihan. 'You ever been on the stage?' he asked.

'No. Often thought I ought to have a go, though. Not very difficult, I imagine. just learning a few lines and prancing about in front of an audience.'

'I was thinking chiefly of production,' Pel said. 'You have a dramatic way of presenting things.'

Le Bihan applied a match to his pipe and began to blow out clouds of blue smoke. In self-defence Pel had to light a cigarette. It was a good excuse.

'So,' Le Bihan went on, 'in the end we decided it *was* done by a car. Even perhaps by something else and disguised to look like a car.'

'And,' Pel said, 'what we have now is rather more than just a suicide.'

'Exactly.' Le Bihan smiled. 'Whichever way you look at it, there seems to have been some criminal intent, and we need to find who did it. For that we need to know who she is.' He beamed at Pel and gestured with his pipe. 'And that,' he ended, 'seems to be where you come in.'

three

The first thing to do was to check with Missing Persons, and that seemed a good job for Sergeant Lagé. Lagé was an amiable, easygoing man who was always willing to do other people's work – usually that of Misset who did as little as possible – so Pel sent him along to see what he could find out.

Missing Persons were inclined to be cynical. It wasn't that they were without hearts, just that, quite apart from those whose disappearances were linked with violence or crime, quite a lot of people chose to vanish for reasons of their own: Men who couldn't stand their wives. Wives who couldn't stand their husbands. Children who couldn't stand their parents. Men whose girl friends had suddenly found themselves in an interesting condition and didn't want to face the obligations. People with debts. People with too much responsibility. People who were sick. People who were too fit for their own good. It kept Missing Persons busy, and, saving their sympathy for anxious relatives, they hadn't a lot to spare for other policemen.

'Of course we've got her here,' Lagé was told cheerfully. 'Together with about ten million others. Disappearing from home's the in thing this year. Got a name?'

'*Part* of a name,' Lagé said. 'Lucie. L.U.C.I.E. We found it on a locket she was wearing round her neck.'

'Where did you find her?'

'In the sea.'

The man behind the desk looked startled. 'Name of God,' he said. 'It's making inroads, isn't it? I've heard of coastal erosion but I didn't know it had got so far inland as Burgundy!'

'Not here,' Lagé explained. 'In Brittany. She probably came from here.'

Files were opened and the computer put to work. 'We have quite a nice selection,' Lagé was informed. 'We have a Lucille Lecesne, for instance. Aged twelve. Disappeared from a farm near Longeau. It's my view she got lost in the woods there and when they find her she'll be dead. Then there's a Marie-Luce Donet, but she's fifty-four; and a Lucianne Charette, but she's got jet-black hair and doesn't sound much like your Lucie. We've also got a kid called Jean-Luc Rouher. On drugs. Aged twenty. Known as "Lucie" to his friends. I think he was one of those. Will he do?'

Lagé gave a pained smile.

'We've got some splendid Anne-Maries and one or two Jeannes. Even a Gabrielle or two. Or how about an Odette?'

Lagé was beginning to show signs of irritation. 'How about cutting out the funny bits?' he suggested. 'She has a scar on her eyebrow, the usual vaccination marks and the marks of a hypodermic on her arm.'

The man behind the desk shrugged. 'Half of them have hypodermic marks on their arm. It's one of the main reasons they go missing. And three quarters have scars along their eyebrows. Where they were hit by a swing as a kid. And they've *all* got vaccination marks. Anything else helpful?'

'She was wearing a dress from Mirabelle's.'

'We don't have files for Mirabelle's? Perhaps you should ask *them*.'

By this time Lagé was beginning to think it might be a good idea.

As they had informed Le Bihan, however, Mirabelle's kept no record of cash sale customers and they'd already been through their records of credit and cheque sales and could produce nothing further. Lagé did his best to describe the dead girl from the information he had but nobody could remember anything.

Trying Narcotics, Lagé then tried to find out if the dead girl were known there, but the result was as uncertain as it had been with Missing Persons. Too little was known about her. They were getting nowhere fast.

Since she'd been found in Concarneau's area, Pel was even beginning by this time to take the view that it was Concarneau's problem not his, especially since his department was busy enough as it was. De Troquereau, who'd been put on to Boyer's missing ducks, had found nothing yet and the Chief was asking questions; the break-in at Talant was still unresolved; and nobody at Noray was talking about the wounding. Noray was a hill village and people in hill villages were inclined to keep their own council so that Misset, who was doing the enquiring and wasn't the most energetic detective in the world, anyway, couldn't have been said to be producing results. However, the death at Marvillers, as Pel had expected, had turned out to be a complicated form of suicide, which was a help, but it still left the assault at Germaine, the petrol theft at Loublanc and the terrorising of the Montchapet district to be sorted out. Le Bihan, he felt, could well search for his dead girl himself but unfortunately the Chief had promised his old friend in Brittany to do all he could.

He was still almost inclined to push the whole thing aside when a thought occurred to him and he pulled forward the photographs Le Bihan had given him. Turning up the one of the necklet, he studied it for a while then rang for Lagé.

'This name,' he said. "Lucie." Perhaps it isn't the name of a girl.'

Lagé looked puzzled. 'Who else's would it be on a locket, Patron? A man's? The necklets men wear are longer and heavier than that. My wife gave me one once. She said she thought it would make me look sexy. All it did was fall in my beer every time I leaned forward.'

Pel gestured. 'When people have names engraved on jewellery for their wives or their girl friends,' he pointed out, 'they usually have it done in decorative lettering, and with some size. The bigger and more flowery the lettering, the more undying the love. Look at this.'

Lagé leaned forward.

'The letters are square Roman-type capitals and they're so minute you can't distinguish them without a magnifying glass. This has been enlarged about ten times. That doesn't sound like a protestation of undying love. Could it be the name of the man who made it? Try Mercier's, the jewellers. They'll probably know.'

Immediately Lagé hit the jackpot. Lagé liked to hit the jackpot occasionally. Though he wasn't blessed with a lot of imagination and didn't have brilliant hunches, he was good at making enquiries because he was always patient and didn't mind taking trouble. Roger Mercier, who ran the family business, recognised the name at once.

'Lucie was well-known,' he said.

'Was?'

'Not any longer.'

Lagé blinked. 'Lucie What, then?'

'Lucie nothing.' Mercier shrugged. 'Just Lucie. The jeweller, Aristide Lucie. He worked here. In this city. In the Rue de Berry.' He began to fish into cupboards and produce dusty books. Laying them in front of Lagé, he explained. 'Look, this is the mark of Tiffanys', of New York: Here's one of Froment-Meurice. Just his name, you see, engraved into his work. This one's Fabergé, in Cyrillic script. Sometime they used their initials. Sometimes their name. Sometimes a monogram or a single letter. Sometimes you also find the city mark – Amsterdam. Paris. Toulouse. Lalique used his surname or his initials. So did Lucie. They were friends and contemporaries, of course, with Lalique perhaps the better. Lucie ran him a good second, though he operated for a much shorter time. I think he made these chains and lockets right up to the time the firm finally packed up.'

'Bankrupt?'

'Oh, no! His son, Georges, was called up for the army like everybody else in 1914 and was killed at Verdun. The only other son, Louis, died in the influenza epidemic in 1918. There was no one else with the skill or knowledge to carry on the business – only an unmarried daughter, Giselle, who had only just started to help in the business – so it just vanished. It doesn't exist any more.'

Lagé sighed. It didn't help much.

Mercier opened another book and showed more photographs. 'There you are,' he said. 'That's one of your chains and lockets. They were rather a speciality of theirs. They made them between 1900 and 1925 when the firm packed up. It's a long time ago, I'm afraid.'

It provided another blank wall but Lagé wasn't patient and hard-working for nothing. He went to the Maire's office and started searching there. Assuming that, if she'd married at all, Giselle Lucie would surely have married somewhere between 1920 and 1930, eventually, in the records for 1922 he turned up a Marie-Joséphine Giselle Lucie, with an address in the city, who had married a man called Marcel Caous. It was a step forward, only a small one, but it *was* forward.

He took the problem back to Roger Mercier who telephoned his father, who was retired, but came up with the information that he'd known a Marcel Caous in the same line of business as himself in Auxerre.

'I don't suppose you know them, do you?' Lagé asked, feeling it was rather a long shot.

'No.' Roger Mercier smiled. 'But, as it happens, I have heard of a Caous. Quite recently, as a matter of fact. She's a girl at the university. My son's there, doing law, and he's been taking her around. I remember remarking on the name.'

Lagé decided there and then that the next time he bought his wife a diamond tiara he'd buy it at Mercier's just to show his appreciation.

Lagé's enquiries at the university revealed three girls with the surname Caous, which surprised everybody at the Hôtel de Police because no one could ever remember the name turning up before, and to find three at once seemed to suggest there was a secret hoard of them somewhere.

Lagé took his discovery to Pel only to find that he was growing a little tired of Le Bihan's dead girl, who seemed to be occupying far too much of his department's time.

'I've been in touch with two of the girls,' Lagé said. 'Both from the Avignay region. They seemed surprised that we'd never heard the name before. Apparently the countryside round there's overrun with people called Caous.'

'Well since we've never heard of them,' Pel said, 'they must be honest.'

They've never heard of Lucies', the jewellers.'

'All square. We've never heard of them; they've never of Lucies'.'

Lagé managed a smile. 'There's still one more – Patricia Caous. I haven't been able to contact her yet. She lives at Tilly-le-Grand, up near Flagey. I've got the address and the telephone number but I got no reply. I asked the police there to try and they say the family's away. Perhaps I should go there myself and enquire.'

'It's not the granddaughter we're looking for,' Pel said shortly. 'It's the grandmother.'

'Yes, Patron.' Lagé hesitated, wondering just what sort of temper Pel was in. 'Is it urgent?'

'Everything done by the Police Judiciaire is urgent,' Pel said coldly. 'But you needn't panic. Had you hoped for a day out at Tilly?'

Lagé *had* been hoping for a day out at Tilly. He'd seen a picture of Patricia Caous in a group photograph at the University and she had proved to be exceptionally pretty, and though Lagé was a happily married man who loved his wife, pretty girls were always pleasant to meet, while a day in the country was even pleasanter. 'No, Patron,' he lied. 'Nothing like that.'

Two days later, having been temporarily side-tracked over a small matter of a break-in at Lorgé and an assault case at Sousmontagne – nothing was ever straightforward in the police and you were never allowed to concentrate for long – he came back to Patricia Caous to find the family had returned. He appeared in Pel's office, delighted with himself.

'The girl at Tilly-le-Grand, Patron,' he said. 'I've contacted her at last. They've been in Italy. She says her great-grand-mother's name before she was married was Giselle Lucie. The grandmother normally lives in Lyons, but at the moment she's staying with her daughter, Madame Edouard Rambeau, the girl's grandmother. Rambeau's managing director of Métaux de Dijon. Address: Manoire de Ramy. I gather she's pretty old. Shall I go to see her?'

'No.' Pel knew what was in Lagé's mind but he felt like a day out of the office himself. 'I'll go.'

The Manoire de Ramy was not a vast house but it was big. Standing in the middle of the village, it was surrounded by a large sloping garden filled with fine old trees and shrubberies and was a little dilapidated, though the dilapidation was not the dilapidation of neglect so much as over-use and, judging by the number of children's bicycles, of over-use by children.

'Mon Dieu, they're not mine,' Madame Rambeau said with a laugh. 'Mine are grown up. I have one in America, one in Paris and one in Avallon. These come from Avallon.'

Her mother, Madame Caous, appeared to have vanished from the face of the earth and excited children were sent in all directions shouting her name.

'She doesn't move very fast these days,' Madame Rambeau pointed out. 'But she gets around.'

'I wouldn't wish to tire her unnecessarily,' Pel said. 'Perhaps you'd like to be present while I talk to her.'

Madame Rambeau laughed. 'She'd be furious. To have her own little secret will make her day. She'll tell us all about it later, of course – many times, I expect.'

Madame Caous emerged eventually from the shrubbery, small, round, frail but with bright, humorous, alert eyes.

'I've been taking a walk in the wood,' she said mildly.

Her daughter looked at her accusingly. 'Doing what, Grandmère?'

'Just doing my exercises. I like to do exercises. Exercises are good for the muscles.' The old lady made a gesture or two with her arms which might or might not have been some sort of Swedish drill.

'You've been smoking,' her daughter accused. 'You know the doctor says you shouldn't.'

'I never smoke,' the old lady said firmly. 'Well, just one after a meal, that's all.'

She had her own small apartment, a sunny corner on the ground floor of the house overlooking the garden, and she led Pel to it, chattering enthusiastically all the time.

'I stay here two months at a time,' she said. 'Then I go to my son in Limoges for two months and then for two months my other son who's in Bordeaux. It keeps me busy and a change is good for the mind. They give me this room so I can see my great-grandchildren. Do you have great-grandchildren, Monsieur Pol?'

'Pel, Madame,' Pel corrected. 'I'm a bit young for great-grandchildren and in any case I'm not married.'

'Oh, you should be, you should be.'

'I hope to be, Madame, before very long.'

'I hope she's nice.' The old lady beamed. 'You look such a kind man, Monsieur Pol. I like being with my descendants. It's good for one's morale. But it does have disadvantages. They're all so strict with me about my diet and my smoking. Do you smoke, Monsieur Pol?'

'Pel, Madame.'

'Of course. Do you?'

'Unfortunately, yes.'

'Have you tried to give it up?'

'Without success, Madame.'

'They say it causes bronchitis, thrombosis and other things.'

Pel leaned forward. Perhaps he could learn something from this splendid old lady, who, despite her smoking, had already arrived at an age which he'd been convinced for years he would never reach.

'What do *you* do about it?' he asked.

'I ignore it,' she said unhelpfully. 'I'm too old to worry. When we were young smoking was fashionable and everybody smoked. Showing off a little, I suppose, Monsieur Pol – '

'Pel, Madame.'

'Of course. So I've smoked all my life and I'm not going to give it up now. Would you like one? Nobody comes in here.'

'What about your daughter? Won't she mind?'

'She'll never know. I blow the smoke up the chimney. Draw your chair nearer.'

For once Pel lit up with a feeling of reassurance. Madame Caous seemed remarkably fit despite her bad habits.

For a moment or two, they happily blew smoke up the chimney then Madame Caous looked up, her eyes bright and interested. 'Do you find it hard trying to give it up, Monsieur Pol?'

'Madame, I find it agonising.'

'They say you put on weight if you stop. I managed it once but it started me eating sweets and taking quick nips at the brandy. I decided I'd exchanged lung cancer for bad teeth and cirrhosis of the liver. Would you like a drink, Monsieur Pol?'

She crossed to a table by the window and returned with a jug of lemonade. 'They make it for me every day,' she explained. 'I don't like it, of course, though the water has a nice bouquet, and it's very good for the intestines.' She smiled over the top of the jug at him. 'But then, everything – even Vichy water – is good for something, isn't it? I often wonder how we manage to die. The only trouble is, it's rather dull and I pour most of it on the flowers.'

Giving Pel a mischievous smile, she half-filled two glasses which she placed on the table. 'Those are for my daughter to find,' she pointed out. 'So she won't ask questions. We'll have my home-made wine.'

Producing two more glasses, she unearthed a dusty bottle from the back of a cupboard and poured two measures. It took Pel's breath away.

'Madame,' he gasped. 'This is powerful stuff.'

She gave a little laugh. 'I add brandy,' she admitted. 'To give it body.'

Pel tried another sip. It made his blood race and sent his temperature soaring but he was thoroughly enjoying himself. It was possible, he decided, to ruin your health and have fun at the same time.

Madame Caous made herself comfortable and looked at him. 'Now, Monsieur Pol, what is it you wanted?'

He explained what he was involved in and asked a few questions about Lucies'. She responded with bright-eyed enthusiasm.

'Our workshop was the best in the region in those days,' she said. 'Certainly in Burgundy. Perhaps even in France. But my brother Georges, who knew everything there was to know about the business, was killed at Verdun. And then Louis died of the Spanish 'flu and that killed my father. I tried to continue but, of course, I hadn't been trained as he had. He knew Lalique and Fabergé. He knew where to find his craftsmen and, when he'd found them, he could talk to them as a craftsman himself.'

Pel produced the photographs he'd obtained from Le Bihan of the necklace worn by the girl found in the sea at Beg Meil. 'Do you recognise that, Madame?' he asked.

She gave a little sigh. 'Of course. These heart necklets were one of our specialities. Like Fabergé's Easter eggs. I sold many of them. Queen Alexandra of England bought one. They were very delicate, and she liked delicate things after the heavy state jewellery she had to wear. The Queen of the Belgians had one also. They're enchanting, don't you think?'

'No more enchanting than you, Madame.' Pel was overcome with gallantry.

She looked up at him, delighted, tiny and frail as Dresden china. 'But like our chains, Monsieur Pol,' she said, 'these days a trifle worn with age.'

'I suppose you've no idea who bought this one?'

'I'm afraid that's impossible. It must be at least sixty years old. We made a great many of them, and many were sold to jewellers in other places. We even exported them – to England and Holland and Spain – and unfortunately there are no longer any records.'

'None at all?'

'They went to the city archives when we closed down and they were destroyed by a bomb during the war. Even so, they wouldn't have revealed who bought our pieces.'

'So there's nothing you can add to what we already know?'

'I'm afraid not, though my memory is really very good when it concerns those days. It's what happened yesterday that I forget. I remember my father and my brothers quite distinctly but I have difficulty recalling my grandchildren. My father was the same. He could remember nothing of the war which killed his son, but he could remember everything of the war of 1870 which took place when he was a young man. It's one of the curiosities of growing old.'

four

Despite the pleasant day out they hadn't moved much further forward, and had found out nothing about the dead girl. Notices and descriptions had been posted outside all police stations and substations but little had come of them. A letter containing all the information they had unearthed to date went off to Inspector Le Bihan and, since their only real clue dated back over half a century, it didn't seem to Pel that they were ever going to be able to help a lot, and he assumed that the query would end up gathering dust and finally, at the bottom of the file of those that remained unanswered, would eventually be forgotten. But two days later Claudie Darel appeared in his office with the morning mail, looking more like a young Mireille Mathieu than ever. Pel smiled at her, he wasn't good at smiling and it made him look as if he were suffering from a migraine, but everybody smiled at Claudie Darel and Pel was no exception.

'Inspector Darcy has a customer,' she said.

Pel glanced at his watch. He had hardly been sitting down more than three minutes and his breakfast – yesterday's croissants and Madame Routy's coffee, which tasted more like paint stripper than an early morning beverage – was still giving him indigestion.

'Already?' he said. 'The shop's only just open.'

'She's from St. Etienne. She came up here yesterday and stayed the night.'

Pel sensed the woman's business might be important. People certainly didn't normally travel from as far as St. Etienne and spend the night in a strange city just for fun.

'Tell Inspector Darcy to send her along.'

As Claudie vanished, Pel rose and walked up and down his office, enjoying the feel of it. It was a new one to go with his promotion. Bigger desk. More comfortable chair. Better carpet – choice of blue, fawn or rust for higher ranks. View over the city these days, too, instead of over the railway track. Even a fan. The people who had designed the Hôtel de Police, having heard of solar heating, had put in large windows to draw as much warmth from the sun as possible to cut down the cost of fuel. Unfortunately, they'd overlooked the fact that the city got more than its fair share of sunshine in a normal summer and the clouds had only to part for an hour for the place to become a greenhouse, so that the police authority had had to dig deep into its pocket to provide fans for its senior officers.

He turned as the door opened. The woman being shown in by Claudie had cold expressionless eyes, a pale face, a mouth as engaging as the peephole in the door of a prison cell and a bosom like the north face of the Eiger.

'Madame Charnier,' Claudie said.

'Sidonie Charnier,' the woman added.

Pel pushed a chair forward. 'Why do you wish to see me?'

'I don't wish to see *you* in particular.' Madame Charnier obviously prided herself on her forthrightness. 'I came to see anybody who could help me. I was taken to see –' she gestured vaguely in the direction of Darcy's office ' – another policeman. He thought you ought to see me. I don't know why *he* couldn't deal with it.'

Sensing difficulties, Pel had fished out a pack of Gauloises and extracted one automatically before he realised what he had done. Guiltily he pushed it back, placed the pack in his

drawer and closed it hurriedly, sitting with his knee against it so he couldn't change his mind.

'You'd better tell me what it's all about,' he said.

'It's about my sister,' Madame Charnier said. 'She's disappeared.'

Immediately Pel knew why Darcy had passed the woman on. Either he suspected the missing sister was Le Bihan's dead woman or he hadn't liked the look of Madame Charnier. Darcy was inclined to be choosy about women.

'Her name, Madame?'

'Pigny. Dominique Pigny. I was Sidonie Pigny before I married.'

'Have you reported her disappearance to Missing Persons?'

'I've only just decided she's disappeared,' Madame Charnier said sharply. 'She hadn't disappeared three weeks ago because I had a letter from her saying she was coming to see me.'

'Age?'

'Thirty-one.'

'Address?'

'I don't have one. She was always on the move and as soon as I'd got one address down, she'd moved to another.'

'Can you describe her?'

'I have photographs.'

There were two photographs, one a studio picture taken in the days when presumably Dominique Pigny had been a little younger, with her hair short and neat and well coiffured. The second had been taken later and was an enlargement of a snapshot. It indicated a young woman who, to put it as mildly as possible, had a roving eye. She was grinning at the camera as if she were daring the photographer into some amorous misadventure – sexy, bold, even dangerous – but the neat coiffure was gone now and the hair was grown long and framed her face like curtains.

'It was taken about a year ago,' Madame Charnier said. 'I had it enlarged. That's how she looked when I saw her last.'

'It seems a good picture,' Pel observed.

'I wouldn't have brought it otherwise,' Madame Charnier said bluntly.

Pel said nothing. Forthrightness, he decided, was sometimes a euphemism for rudeness. He sat back and drew a deep breath. 'You'd better tell me about her.'

'She was a drop-out,' Madame Charnier said in matter-of-fact tones. 'I can't think why she was affected like this. I never was.' Pel could well believe it. 'We were well brought up at home. Strictly even. My parents demanded responsibility. My children are the same. I believe in obedience and duty. If there were more of it, there'd be less crime.'

Pel was entirely in agreement but he had a feeling that Madame Charnier's idea of obedience and duty would have made her a better cop than a mother.

'She never seemed to settle,' she went on. 'She was clever but she never did anything with her ability.'

'Was she unhappy?'

Madame Charnier frowned. 'Anything but. It was disgusting the way she lived. She had no conscience. She was wild. Sometimes I even wondered if she were unbalanced.'

'Why?'

'She once got a job as cook on a trawler out of Concarneau.'

'Concarneau?'

Pel's mind immediately started clicking away like mad because Concarneau was only a few kilometres from Beg Meil.

'We were born in Quimper and lived there until my father's job took him to St. Etienne. I was fifteen. She was a year younger. She worked in a circus for a while. She even tried drugs. Soft drugs first. Those cigarettes they smoke. She tried to get me to have a go, but I refused.'

'You were very wise, Madame.'

'Eventually, she tried heroin.' Madame Charnier looked up and Pel saw her eyes were unsympathetic and he wondered why she was so concerned. 'But she overcame it. She was arrested in Valence for stealing. She worked for an antique dealer and, because she needed money for drugs, she stole a silver goblet and tried to sell it. When she was caught, it frightened her and she agreed to take a course to overcome the habit. She did, of course. I'll admit that. When she set her mind on a thing, she always succeeded.'

'Where was she living?'

Madame Charnier shrugged. 'I don't know. In this area, I think.' Once she mentioned Arne, and there's an Arne on the way to Langres. I looked it up.'

'Do you think she was living there?'

'All she said was something about going there. Some man, I expect. She was always after men. But I didn't hear her properly and when I asked what she'd said, she pretended she hadn't said anything.'

'Did she ever mention Arne again?'

'No. And she always posted her letters in different places. They were postmarked Dijon. Or Châtillon. Or Langres. All this area, but always different. As if she were deliberately hiding from me.'

'Why would she do that?'

Madame Charnier sniffed. 'She never wanted to be part of the normal decent life. I often tried to tell her about her behaviour but she'd never listen. She left home originally because she quarrelled with my parents' discipline. When they died within a few months of each other she stayed with me for a while, but all the time she seemed to be driven by the wish to be different from everybody else. She resented people interfering. It caused rows. At home we called her

Dominique la Panique. But she kept in touch. Telephone calls. Letters. Always cheerful. Only someone unaware of the meaning of sin could have been like that. And then – ' Madame Charnier frowned and sat up straighter ' – then three weeks ago she telephoned to say she was coming home. She said she wanted to talk.'

'What did she mean by home?'

'*My* home. When our parents died, I took over the house, of course.'

'By agreement with your sister?'

'There was no question of an agreement. I was married, she wasn't, so it became mine.'

'Were you looking forward to the visit?'

Madame Charnier frowned. 'She was a troublemaker.'

'In what way?'

'She tried to take my husband from me.'

'What happened?'

'I hit her. She left him alone after that.'

'And your husband?'

'He came home.'

Pel didn't pursue the line. It wasn't hard to believe that Madame Charnier had enough power of personality to have persuaded her erring husband it would be wiser to mend his ways.

'So. It seems there isn't much love lost between you, Madame. Why do you wish her to be found?'

Madame Charnier looked at him coldly. 'Because she's my sister and it's my duty. Besides, she owed me money.'

'Much?'

'I lent her some to live on. I never saw it again and I suppose now I never shall.'

'But she *was* coming home? Despite this business with your husband? You forgave her?'

'No. It was just my duty not to abandon her. For some reason, my children liked her. She was good with them, I admit. Perhaps she should have had one of her own.'

'Had she any men friends at the moment?'

'I think there was one.'

'Do you know where he came from?'

'Somewhere over in the north-west, she said.' Madame Charnier's hand gestured vaguely.

'Brittany for instance?'

'It might have been.'

'Did *she* ever go back to Brittany, Madame? After you left there. Apart from this job she took?'

'We used to go back there in August. My parents took a house.'

'At Beg Meil?' Or Concarneau? That area.'

'No. Further east at Carnac.'

'But she knew Brittany?'

'I suppose so. Though we stopped going there before I married.'

'Had she been back recently?'

'I think she had. My children received a postcard a few months ago from Concarneau. But she was always moving about. There was also one from Lyons. Why do you ask?'

Pel sighed. 'Could you describe her, Madame? Apart from the photographs.'

'She looked a little like me. Same colouring. Same skin. But she looked a lot younger. I don't know how she did it, the life she led.' Madame Charnier seemed to be considering the unfairness of fate. 'She was slimmer, of course, and smaller.'

'About one hundred and sixty centimetres?'

'About that. I'm a hundred and sixty-four.' Madame suddenly looked like a bird dog that had found a scent. 'You know where she is?'

Pel held up a hand and fished in his drawer for copies of the photographs Inspector Bihan held. He rejected the ones of the dead girl and instead laid the one of the Lucie necklet on the desk.

'Do you know this necklet, Madame?'

Madame Charnier frowned. 'Yes,' she said.

'Was it your sister's?'

'I saw her wearing it.'

'Do you know where she got it?'

'Some man, I expect. It looks expensive. More expensive than she could afford. More than I could afford. *Is* it expensive?'

'I would say yes.'

Madame Charnier shrugged, then suddenly woke up to what the necklet implied, as if it had slipped past her notice until that second. 'Where is this necklet?' she asked. 'Why isn't she wearing it now? Where's my sister?'

Pel drew a deep breath. 'I think, Madame,' he said slowly, 'that your sister is dead.'

five

Pel was feeling a little worn when he called Darcy in. Madame Charnier had borne the news she'd received without emotion. It was almost as if she'd been expecting something of the sort and regarded it as just retribution for a sinful life.

Against all the rules he'd been trying to force on himself, he opened his drawer and extracted a cigarette. The hardest part of police work, he decided, wasn't necessarily facing armed criminals.

He drew on the cigarette for a while, convinced it was another nail in his coffin. 'Know anything about Arne?' he asked slowly.

'A bit,' Darcy said. 'I met a girl once who came from round there. Next village, I think it was – Violette. I drove her home a few times. It's on the edge of the hills. Near Châtillon. Agricultural. Cattle chiefly. Only around a hundred or two inhabitants. Plus the château.'

'What château?'

'Château d'Ivry. Home of the Comte d'Ivry de Queyel.'

'Is he still there?'

'Not unless he haunts the corridors after midnight. He was topped during the revolution. Since then various people have owned it.'

Pel looked at the sky. 'It's a nice day,' he said innocently. 'Fancy a drive?'

If there hadn't been a place like Burgundy, Pel thought placidly as the drove northwards from the city, then surely someone would have had to invent it. Without rivers or coastline to border it, it wasn't immediately distinguishable from its neighbours and most people thought of it only as a wine. But, he felt, if Paris was the face of France then Burgundy was surely the heart, a generous region that made the rest of France superfluous.

The sun was hot when they arrived at Arne and, being in no hurry since they were making enquiries only on behalf of Le Bihan, they sat on the pavement outside the local bar and sank a couple of cool beers. Over the houses to the north, they could see the turrets of the château. It was of grey stone, with round fairy-tale towers, and it stood on a ridge of land, looking almost artificial as it lifted above the village. It was surrounded by trees with, below, running alongside the River Ives, lush meadows filled with fat cattle.

'Who lives there now?' Pel asked.

'Some old boy,' Darcy said. 'Name of Stocklin. Charles-Louis Stocklin. Million years old. Worth a fortune. Bought it about ten years ago.'

They tried the pictures of Dominique Pigny on the proprietor of the bar but he shook his head. 'She never came here,' he said. 'I'd have remembered her if she had. I always remember the pretty ones.'

The Curé had also never seen her, and she'd never been noticed in the shops. Since the shops consisted only of a butcher's, a baker's and a general store it wasn't surprising. Anyone as enterprising as Dominique Pigny had been would surely have gone further afield for her purchases. As a last resort they tried the château.

The man who opened the door was around forty, tall, strong, square-faced and blond with the look of a German. He wore a white jacket and, showing them in, disappeared down the hall calling 'Bernadine.'

'She runs the place,' he said.

The woman was tall and blonde like the man, well-built and good-looking with an excellent figure. Leading them into a panelled room flooded with sunshine that came through tall mullioned windows, she indicated chairs.

'I'm Bernadine Guichet,' she said. 'I'm the housekeeper. My brother, Hubert, is the butler. Or at least that's what he's called. He's really just a handyman. I do the cooking and the nursing and he does the lifting and the heavy chores. We look after Monsieur Stocklin between us. He's bedridden these days.'

'Isn't it a hard job looking after an old man?' Pel asked.

She smiled. 'It's better than working in a hospital. We no longer have a family home to go to and this is a pleasant enough place to live. We thought it might be nice one day to open a home for old people.'

Studying the pictures Pel offered, copies of those Madame Charnier had produced, her face betrayed no sign of recognition, either of the girl or the necklet.

'Name of Pigny,' Pel said. 'Dominique Pigny.'

'Nobody by that name ever worked here. Not while we've been here.'

'And how long would that be?'

'Two years. We came from the south.'

'What other staff have you?'

'My brother and I look after everything.'

'In a place this size?'

'There's only Monsieur Stocklin. He doesn't demand much.'

Pel looked through the window. Below them, the valley, running alongside the river, stretched away to the north. It was reached by a path from the house.

'What about Monsieur Stocklin?' he asked. 'Would he know her?'

Bernadine Guichet gave a small tight smile. 'I doubt it very much. He doesn't read the newspapers and he stays all the time in his room. Hubert and I have an apartment close by so we can hear if he needs anything. Very little happens here – certainly nothing to attract a young girl. The only traffic's from the village to Violette or to Mercourt and Mongy on the way to Langres. Otherwise just an occasional car.'

'What outside staff do you have?'

'One farm foreman – the farm's further down the slope – and two men. We raise beef cattle which require little looking after. They used to grow potatoes and other crops but, with Monsieur Stocklin no longer able to take much interest, it was decided to cut everything to the simplest form and that part's been closed down.'

Pel was inclined to be silent on the way back. Old people bothered him because he had a feeling he was going to become an old person himself at any moment and had no wish to be neglected. His own father had obligingly dropped dead at the age of seventy-nine in the garden of his younger daughter in Châtillon, and though Pel had always been terrified of him because his temper was, if anything, worse than Pel's, he had admired the manner of his going because it had been as neat and efficient as his life.

'Old age's a big problem,' he said. 'What do you do with old people?'

Darcy shrugged. 'Tie them to the railway line. Leave them in a refuse bin at the side of the motorway. Seal them up in the nose cone of a rocket and fire them into outer space.'

'One day you'll be old.' Pel spoke with the bitterness of one already on the threshold.

'Not me, Patron. I shall die of a heart attack while trying to grab a villain or bed a woman. Daniel Darcy, with his death-defying coronary.'

To Pel, Darcy's attitude was too flippant. 'What about *your* father?' he asked.

'Still alive.'

'Does *he* chase girls too?'

Darcy grinned. 'He's worse than me.'

When they reached the Hôtel de Police, Pel sent Cadet Martin out for a bottle of beer for him, and sat brooding over the photographs Madame Charnier had left with them. For some reason the dead girl bothered him. If nothing else, she must have had a personality, and it seemed strange that nobody had ever noticed her except her sister who had managed only to disapprove of her.

Ringing for Cadet Martin, he handed him the pictures. 'Have those copied,' he said. 'We'll need them for the press. It's the sort of story they thrive on.'

Battle, murder and sudden death were like meat and drink to the newspapers these days and a story was hardly worth printing unless somebody had been killed or maimed. He could just see the headlines.

Considering all things, he wasn't too disappointed with the day as he climbed into his car and headed for his home in the Rue Martin-de-Noinville. They hadn't discovered much but they'd had a pleasant afternoon out.

His car was giving trouble again. It limped round the Place Wilson and down the Cours de Gaulle, smoke pouring from the exhaust. Near the Monument de la Victoire he was held up by traffic and a van driver alongside, pulling a face at the fumes, opened his window and leaned out.

'Why don't you use petrol, mon vieux?' he asked. 'Or else smokeless coal?'

Pel scowled. It was no good, he thought. The car would have to go – it humiliated him too often – and he started doing sums in his head. For weeks he'd surreptitiously been looking at advertising material for new cars but every time he made up his mind what to buy, the accompanying price list made him change his mind.

Madame Routy was sitting in a deckchair behind the house. Where she sat was known to Pel as the 'terrasse' but, in fact, it was nothing more than a narrow strip of concrete bordering a handkerchief lawn. The next door neighbour was in a deckchair on her own 'terrasse' and they were conducting their conversation in shouts.

Pel glared at her. She ought, he felt, to have been leafing through cookery books in the kitchen in order to prepare some magnificent repast for his delectation. Instead, he supposed, it would be the usual casserole: three or four chunks of meat – chop-chop and into the dish; a few vegetables – chop-chop and after the meat. A shake of pepper and salt and that would be what Madame Routy blithely called preparing a meal. Madame Routy, he decided, was going to get a shock when he finally got Madame Faivre-Perret before the Maire for the marriage ceremony.

'Fancy a game of boules?'

Pel turned at the voice and beamed at the boy who stuck his head round the kitchen door. Didier Darras was Madame Routy's nephew and usually turned up at Pel's when his mother went to look after an ailing father-in-law.

They shook hands gravely.

'Grandfather ill again?' Pel asked.

Didier shrugged. 'I think he likes being ill,' he said. 'He gets better food when Maman goes over there.'

'When you come over here, mon vieux, I'll bet you don't get better food.'

Didier grinned. He was growing into a sturdy strong boy. 'We could always eat out,' he said.

Pel grinned back conspiratorially. Didier was the only ally he possessed against Madame Routy. He disliked her food and regarded television in much the same manner as Pel, and their chief delight was to disappear to play boules or go fishing just as she started cooking then forget to return so that she had to eat her disgusting dishes herself.

'I would have imagined,' Pel said, 'that by this time you'd have learned to cook.'

The boy's shoulders moved. 'You know such good restaurants,' he grinned. 'In any case, I've not come to stay. I'm going home to sleep. I'm not scared of being alone and Louise Bray next door says her parents are going out so I can go round there if I want.' He paused, his face thoughtful. 'People often marry the girl next door, don't they?'

It had been Pel's experience that more often than not they didn't, for the simple reason that they knew too much about them. 'Are you thinking of getting married, mon brave?' he asked.

'Oh, yes. Eventually. But not just yet. What about you? When are *you* getting married?'

'Why do you ask?'

'Aunt Routy says it's getting near.'

Nearer than you imagine, mon brave, Pel thought.

'We're coming over here next week,' Didier went on. 'Me and Louise. There's no school and we thought we'd cycle to Drax and have a look at the caves.'

'Take care,' Pel advised. 'The caves at Drax need to be approached with trepidation. Potholers regularly risk their necks trying to reach the bowels of the earth there and equally regularly the police are called on to fish them out when they get stuck.'

Didier gestured. 'We're not exploring,' he said. 'And the first hundred yards are quite safe. And this is a good time to go. There's never anybody there until August.'

The following morning, Pel appeared at the Hôtel de Police with a smug expression on his face. With the aid of Didier Darras, he had defeated Madame Routy once again. They had not only failed to turn up to eat the meal she had prepared, but had later played Scrabble in the kitchen with such gusto she had complained she couldn't hear the television. Considering that it was shuddering on its stand, they had had to assume she was stone deaf. It was a victory as resounding as Austerlitz.

He found Claudie Darel in his office. She looked white and unhappy and her expression put him on the alert at once.

'What's wrong?'

'Patron, I think you've had a letter bomb. Régis Martin and I were going through the mail and we came across this parcel about the size of a book. When I started to open it I saw wires.'

'Where is it now?'

'Still on the desk. I came in here to warn you. Régis is guarding the door until we've had it checked. The army's sending an explosives expert from the barracks.'

Cadet Martin was standing in the doorway of the office he shared with Claudie, looking a little pale but full of determination. 'It very nearly got us, Patron,' he said.

Pel approached the desk carefully, his head down like a dog sniffing for a scent. The parcel was on the desk, one end half-opened. Without touching it, he peered at it. What Claudie had said was true. There were wires.

When the explosives people arrived, they removed it carefully and defused it.

'Pretty simple,' the army sergeant said. 'Plastic torch case. Battery taking up half the space, the other half filled with explosive. It could blind you or blow your hand off.' He looked up at Darcy and Pel. 'Got any enemies who'd like to do that to you?'

'Yes,' Darcy snapped. 'Philippe Duche.'

When the soldiers had taken away the defused bomb, Darcy sat down at the opposite side of Pel's desk and pushed across a packet of cigarettes.

Pel took one. 'Perhaps under the circumstances,' he agreed.

Darcy lit it for him. 'This is a new one, Patron.'

Pel shrugged. 'The world these days is ready-made for crackpots.'

'Philippe Duche isn't a crackpot, Patron.'

'I'm not afraid of Philippe Duche,' Pel snorted.

'I am. You'll be no good to us without eyes and hands. Leave it to me, Patron. I'll get the bastard. I know his haunts. Can you manage without me?'

Pel smiled. 'I doubt it, Daniel. But I'll try, and things are quiet at the moment.'

Darcy frowned. 'I'll use Lacocq and Morell. We can't have tinpot little villains trying to remove cops just because they happened to catch the bastards doing something dishonest and sent them for a well-deserved rest behind bars.' He gestured indignantly. 'The nerve of the bastard! He tries to take over a city and then, when he's caught, he resents it. Just forget it, Patron. I'll make it my job.'

As Darcy bustled off, his face angry, Pel sat for a moment in silence. Darcy was right, of course. They couldn't let villains go around committing mayhem for revenge and getting away with it. Curiously, it wasn't for himself that he was angry, but at the thought of what might have happened to Claudie Darel, who was young and pretty and had all her life before her.

As he came to life and began to paw through the papers on his desk, he came across the typed sheets containing the information Madame Charnier had given him. He frowned at them. Death was never easy, even when it wasn't your own, and Dominique Pigny had been unceremoniously dumped in the sea by someone who had killed her – accidentally, with a car; or somewhat less accidentally because he'd made her pregnant. Probably a man who came, in Madame Charnier's words, from 'somewhere in the north-west,' which doubtless meant Brittany and more than likely somewhere round Beg Meil where she'd been found.

However, with Madame Charnier disappearing to Brittany to identify her sister's body, their part in the affair seemed to be ended. They had shown efficiency, nose-to-the-grindstone and eye-on-the-ball and, since whatever had happened appeared to have happened in Brittany, it seemed now to be entirely Inspector Le Bihan's business. At least the press wouldn't be clamouring at his door.

But, as with Darcy and Nosjean, that was where Pel was wrong, too.

six

The bomb had shaken the Hôtel de Police a little. Despite the resentment about their existence that was felt in some circles, they weren't in the habit of receiving explosives in their mail.

Pel himself was under no delusions. He wasn't treating Philippe Duche's threat lightly. 'But I can hardly lock myself in,' he pointed out.

'Fair enough, Patron,' Darcy agreed. 'But I think you should start looking under your car when you go to it in the morning. And make sure your doors and windows are locked and close the shutters at night.'

Uniformed Branch was already putting on a big search of the city and its environs. Barns, store sheds and old houses were being checked and policemen were asking questions wherever they would be most useful. So far, however, nothing had been turned up to indicate that Philippe Duche hadn't sunk without trace.

'He's gone into the hills,' Inspector Nadauld, of Uniformed Branch, decided.

'More likely to Paris,' was the opinion of Inspector Pomereu, of Traffic, who had been manning road blocks and searching cars. 'They all go to Paris. You could hide an army in Paris.'

Darcy's view was that Philippe Duche was still in the city. He was a single-minded individual, and if he'd said he was going to get Pel, then he'd undoubtedly try.

His first move was to have all the apartments and offices overlooking the Hôtel de Police checked to make sure their occupants were good citizens and not friends or associates of Philippe Duche, and to make sure that Pel's home couldn't be overlooked from neighbouring houses or from the bank of the railway line which ran nearby. Then he arranged with Uniformed Branch to keep an eye on the place. Finally he made enquiries in Benois de l'Herbue, a narrow-gutted village south of the city just off the N74, where Philippe Duche had been born and grown up. He hadn't been seen there recently but Darcy guessed he'd been there, visiting his father who kept a small bar just off the main square. The Duche family carried a lot of weight in Benois de l'Herbue and people weren't prepared to say anything, but Darcy was quick to notice the fleetingly scared looks on their faces as they answered his questions. Moving quietly, making no fuss, it didn't take him long to learn that Duche was in the Montchapet district of the city. He nodded quietly, lit a cigarette and climbed back into his car. Darcy was a lively young man, modern as a spacecraft and, when it came to girls, just as efficient, but he was a good policeman, too. Girls didn't interfere with his work when he was on a job and he was in deadly earnest at that moment. At times, he felt like sinking a hatchet into Pel's skull but he knew he was a good policeman and, since there weren't many like him, he deserved to be looked after.

For the rest of Pel's team life followed the usual pattern of enquiry and arrest – or of enquiry and non-arrest. The break-in at the supermarket at Talant had been sorted out with a brisk reminder to the management that it was about time they put a new set of locks on their doors. The wounding at Noray was still a mystery – though doubtless the result of jealousy over a girl – but the terrorists of the Montchapet district had turned out to be nothing more than a gang of unruly fourteen-year-olds. The department was making headway and they were just congratulating themselves that in the statistics for the year the column indicating the number of crimes solved would show a no-worse-than-average rate when the balance was tipped again by a woman called Argoud from Roumy who was brought in for severely wounding her husband with a brass candlestick by hitting him over the head while he lay asleep in bed, and Misset, who had taken the call from the neighbours, was at that moment searching for the man's mistress. Misset felt he knew something about these things, because he'd fancied a mistress or two himself for ages. Since Madame Argoud was refusing to talk and had sat in sullen silence throughout the whole questioning, Misset could only assume that this was because she was refusing to name the other woman. There *had* to be another woman, he felt. There always was.

With the Argoud woman safely in the hands of the juge d'instruction, he had returned to the case at Noray but he didn't seem to be trying very hard and Pel suspected that, with Noray a long way from the eyes of a superior officer and Lagé doing all the hard work, Misset was probably enjoying himself.

Misset would have to be pulled up sharply again, Pel decided. Misset spent most of his career being pulled up sharply. Misset was like that. His marriage produced a lot of children but not much love and Pel regularly heard of girls in the typing pool complaining of his attentions.

De Troquereau, meanwhile, was still absorbed with Boyer's missing ducks. Cholley was little more than a hamlet that rarely saw a car, and Boyer's poultry were all over the dusty road, together with two pigs and a couple of dogs drowsing in the sunshine. Boyer's wife was a cheerful matronly woman free with the wine who was more than taken with De Troquereau. He was slight, neatly built, and handsome, and she'd discovered somehow that he was a baron – Charles-Victor De Troquereau Tournay-Turenne. Because he was as poor as a church rat, De Troq' tended to keep quiet about his title and she felt his reticence was the innate modesty of a born aristocrat, something which could hardly be true when you considered the car he drove, an open tourer with a belt across the bonnet and headlamps like searchlights.

'They were my ducks rather than my husband's,' she told him. 'It's always the tradition that the farmer's wife has the poultry for pin money.'

She led De Troq' across the dusty farmyard into a field where there were three huts, two containing laying hens, the third empty and with a hole in the side where boards had been levered off.

'That's where he got in,' she said.

'Was it this chap, Jeanneny, do you think?'

She laughed. 'Of course not, mon brave,' she said. 'He just once put one across my husband over a cow he sold, and my husband's never forgiven him.'

'Were the ducks always put up here?'

'Every night at 7.30. There's a pond at the end of the field. They have to have water. Ducks are a bit special. They like to forage for grass and worms and they don't take kindly to the intensive breeding and laying you can go in for with hens.'

'Valuable?'

She drew herself up. 'They're thoroughbreds. Indian Runners. Dark brown. Stand upright like penguins. Bred for laying. They can produce up to three hundred eggs a year.' She smiled at De Troq'. 'Find me those ducks,' she said, 'and you'll get half a dozen bottles of the finest wine we've got. And I've got a brother with a vineyard south of Beaune.'

De Troq' smiled back. 'We're not allowed to take gifts,' he said.

Madame Boyer laughed. 'I'm not offering gifts, mon brave,' she said. 'It's a good honest bribe.'

Pel had not told Madame Faivre-Perret about Duche's threat and the arrival of the letter bomb and they had managed to keep it out of the newspapers. For all Duche knew, it was still hanging about the Hôtel de Police waiting to blow Pel's head off and it was better that he should be kept guessing so he wouldn't send another. It didn't suit Pel not to tell Madame but he didn't wish to worry her unnecessarily, because she actually seemed to relish the idea of being married to him. It was something he still found hard to understand because, studying himself in the mirror as he shaved, he couldn't see what she saw in him.

Didier had disappeared but so, thank God, had Madame Routy. While visiting her sister, she had gone down with some sort of plague which was confining her to bed, and a message had been sent via the next door neighbour. Since Pel had felt obliged to inform her of the letter bomb when he'd instructed her not to touch any mail that arrived, he suspected she'd got the wind up.

He could hardly blame her – handling bombs wasn't the métier of a middle-aged housekeeper. But, if nothing else, it meant that – bliss! – Pel had the house to himself, without the television roaring away all the time like a jumbo taking off, and with the 'confort anglais' free whenever he wanted it. It meant providing his own breakfast, of course, even an occasional meal later in the day when Madame Faivre-Perret was too occupied with her business affairs to offer one. But that was easily overcome. For his breakfast he stood, as he'd stood on and off for years, at the counter of the Bar Transvaal opposite the Hôtel de Police with a coffee and a croissant while, on Darcy's orders, Aimedieu kept an eye on the rest of the custom just in case. For the other meals he existed on tins of tripes à la mode de Caen – bought not by himself but on Darcy's instructions by Cadet Martin at a city supermarket – which were infinitely better, despite coming out of tins, than anything Madame Routy cooked.

Despite the threat hanging over him, he was well content. Only his smoking troubled him. Millions of other people stopped smoking. Why couldn't he? Madame Faivre-Perret's decorous salutations, he felt, must seem to her like kissing an ash tray. Besides, it cost him a fortune. Without it he would smell sweeter and have more money in his pocket, and, with the amount of carbon monoxide he absorbed, he might just as well stick a car exhaust up his nostrils.

He had even taken the trouble to write for a pamphlet the government had issued to help people. Its chief suggestion was to throw away his cigarettes and as advice *that* was a dead loss, because no sensible Burgundian could be expected to throw away something he'd paid good money for. He would either have to get someone to knock him on the head or accept that he was going to end up cancerous, arthritic, asthmatic, blind, deaf and stupid.

The morning was occupied with studying the newspapers. Pel always liked to know what they were thinking. Under French law, they were allowed to make comments on police cases and most of them were quite uninhibited about matters that were sub judice, making wild statements and generally pointing an accusing finger in the wrong direction. However, there *were* times when they were helpful because Pel had long since noticed that a leak to them printed across the front page at a time when he could expect a criminal he was after to be still a little nervous could lead to panic, which never failed to be a help.

Martin had laid the newspapers on his desk, all the relevant items ringed with red pencil. Martin liked to think himself a good judge of what Pel ought to see and behaved at times like the editor of *France Soir*. They carried all the latest scores for murder, arson, extortion, embezzlement, breaking and entering, sedition, pimping, offences against public morals, robbery with violence, cruelty to children, bombs, acid throwing, sale of drugs to minors, adulteration of foods, counterfeiting, smuggling, perjury, incitement to desertion, and non-assistance to persons in danger. They also all carried the photographs of the Pigny girl across the front page, *Le Bien Public* with a certain amount of discretion, *France Soir* filling almost half the page with trumpeting headlines: DEAD GIRL'S MYSTERY LIFE. WHERE DID SHE SPEND HER DAYS?

What they'd discovered – or failed to discover – from Arne had been sent to Inspector Le Bihan and that, Pel felt, was the end of his part in the affair. He was very surprised, therefore, when he returned from lunch with Judge Polverari to find a note on his desk from Cadet Martin.

'Substation at Mongy telephoned,' it said. 'Please ring Brigadier Bardolle. Urgent. Pigny Case.'

Picking up the telephone, Pel asked for Mongy. The weather was warm again and his lunch had been a good one so that he was almost drowsing when the telephone came to life.

'MONGY! BRIGADIER BARDOLLE!'

Bardolle had the vocal cords of a loud-hailer and nobody, it seemed, had ever instructed him in the use of the telephone. His bellow left Pel with ringing ears.

Holding the receiver well away from his head, he answered quietly in the hope that his example would be followed, but Bardolle didn't seem to catch on and went on in the same iron voice, as if he were on the bridge of a ship hailing the shore.

'Those pictures in the paper,' he said. 'Of that Pigny girl. I've had a man in here who says he knows her.'

Pel sat up. 'He does? Who is he?'

'Type who runs the bar. She was with a man in his place a month ago.'

'A month ago!' Pel's eyebrows shot up. This made things different! If she were seen in Mongy only a month before, that mystery life of hers the newspapers were wondering about had probably been conducted somewhere near Mongy. And anywhere near Mongy was a good place to conduct a mystery life, because Mongy was close to Arne and was lost in an area north-east of the city full of deep valleys and thick woods. It was populated chiefly by a farming community which minded its own business, and was just the sort of place that a girl like Dominique Pigny, who seemed to prefer to live her life in her own way, would choose. And if she'd been seen with a man in the local bar, it was more than likely that *he*, not someone in Brittany, had been responsible for her death. The news threw the ball squarely into Pel's court.

Calling for Aimedieu, who had been told by Darcy never to take his eyes off Pel, he stuffed notebook and pencils into his pocket and followed them with a spare packet of Gauloises in case he finished the one already on his person. Avoid situations where he would want to smoke, the government pamphlet had said. As a policeman, there was a fat chance of anything like that.

As Aimedieu swung the car out of the Rue de la Liberté and round the Porte Guillaume, a couple of pedestrians did a hop, skip and jump for the pavement.

'You nearly got those two,' Pel said dryly.

Aimedieu's choirboy face was expressionless. 'It keeps them on their toes, Patron,' he said.

'What happens if you hit them?'

'They're a lot quicker next time. It's different here from Paris, of course. Here it's just a sport. In Paris, they *expect* to be knocked down.'

Despite his innocent looks, Pel decided, Aimedieu was quite a wit.

As they roared down from the Langres plateau into Drax, Pel remembered Didier and realised that this was the day when he'd arranged to take his girl friend, Louise Bray, to the caves. Doubtless there was more than merely geology about the dark interior to interest them.

Mongy was some distance further on, situated in a deep valley surrounded by woods. With the afternoon sun on it, it was not just warm, it was hot. The police substation, a flat-fronted building flying the tricolour over the doorway, was just off the main square, the entrance up a short flight of steps. Inside was a desk and a switchboard manned by a policeman. Pel knew they'd arrived at the right spot at once because he could hear a voice that twanged like a banjo coming from an office along the corridor. Every word was clear.

'Look,' it was saying, 'it doesn't matter what your client says. The wheels were missing and the tyres were found on your client's car... Of course I can identify them. He'd just had two of them replaced. He'd ordered them from the garage here and they'd written his name on them for when he left his car. In yellow chalk. It was still there when I found them. Your client ought to get glasses.'

'Brigadier Bardolle?' Pel said to the man behind the desk.

The policeman nodded. 'He's busy,' he said. 'A tyre stealing case. He's talking to a lawyer in Châtillon.'

Pel sniffed. 'Why doesn't he use the telephone?' he asked.

Bardolle brought his conversation to a close, slammed the telephone down on its rest with a crash that suggested it had been left in pieces, and appeared in the corridor, glowering and muttering to himself. He had a figure that went with his voice because he was almost as wide as he was high, with a chest like a brewery dray, and deep-set pale blue eyes under heavily scowling eyebrows. He reminded Pel a little of Dr. Frankenstein's monster.

'Stupid con,' he was muttering. 'Thinking we'd fall for a story like that.' As he saw Pel he brightened up. 'Chief

Inspector,' he said in his tremendous iron voice. 'Recognised you straight away!'

His smile of welcome changed his whole face. From being a hobgoblin out of a horror story he became the sort of policeman whose arms children swung on as he saw them across the road.

'This man – ' Pel began.

'Got him right here, sir! Well, not here. just along the street. Fifty yards from this very spot. Bar Giorgiou.'

Pel glanced at Aimedieu. 'Bar Giorgiou 8 p.m.,' the letter found in Dominique Pigny's pocket had said. They seemed to have struck gold.

'Norbert Hilaire,' Bardolle was saying. 'Old soldier. Like me. Straight as they come. He won't have you on.'

'He'd better not,' Pel said.

Bardolle looked at his watch. 'Just come right, too,' he said. 'Heat of the afternoon. Cold beer would go down well.'

The bar was cool and Norbert Hilaire looked just what Bardolle had said he was. He was teak-faced and his back was straight and, like Bardolle, he had the stature of a carthorse. Harnessed together, they wouldn't have looked amiss pulling a plough.

He gestured to a table and, as they sat down, he appeared alongside them with four cold beers.

'This girl – ' Pel began.

Hilaire glanced at Bardolle. 'I saw her picture and went along to see Gabriel here.'

Pel looked at Bardolle. Somehow he didn't look like a Gabriel. More like an Achille or a Ulysse. A Ferdinand at the very least.

'We're old friends,' Hilaire went on. 'He was the first guy I thought of.'

'And the girl?'

'Well, I'm certain it's the one whose picture was in the paper.'

'Do you know her well?'

'No. I only saw her once. But it was a night when there was nothing doing and I had plenty of chance to study her. These two were the only people in the place and they were here a long time. They had a meal. We do omelettes and chicken and things like that. They arrived about eight o'clock.'

'Are you *certain* it was this girl?' Pel laid the pictures Madame Charnier had given him on the table.

Hilaire studied them carefully. 'Certain,' he said.

'Did you hear her name?' Pel asked.

'Only her first name.'

'Which was?'

'The man called her Dominique.'

Pel nodded, satisfied he was on the right track. 'Did you hear what they were talking about?'

'Not really,' Hilaire said. 'I wasn't listening. But I couldn't help hearing bits. They seemed to be quarrelling.'

'What about?'

'I don't know. She seemed to be wanting him to do something and he didn't seem to want to.'

'Did you hear the man's name?'

'No.' Hilaire frowned, trying to cast his mind back. 'I don't think she ever called him by his proper name. At least, not so that I could hear. I got the impression that he'd been her boy friend, perhaps living with her, and she'd given him up. That's what I thought, but I might be wrong. It might have been some other guy.'

'Did they mention Brittany?'

'In what way?'

'Going there. Visiting it. Something like that.'

'I didn't hear them.'

'Had she a suitcase with her?'

'I didn't see one.'

'Did either of them mention Beg Meil?'

'Not to my knowledge.'

'Any other names?'

'I heard the man say something about his house at Villiers.'

Pel looked at Bardolle. 'There's a Villiers round here somewhere, isn't there?'

'That's right. Villiers-sur-Orche. Just to the north. My cousin runs the substation there. Brigadier Delhaye.'

The backwoods of Burgundy were like the backwoods of Brittany, it seemed. Everybody was related.

'We'd better have a few enquiries made there,' Pel said.' 'What was this man like?'

'Big type. Hair on the long side. Broad shoulders, a bit stooping. Looked as though a couple of extra years in the army would have done him good. And temper? More than once I thought I ought to throw them out before they started hurling the crockery at each other. But they always seemed to calm down just before they got to that stage and even started smiling at each other. Weird? You ought to have seen them.'

'What about the girl?'

'She was doing all the talking and he seemed to be doing all the listening.'

'Anything else you can remember about him? Something we could use to identify him. Did he have a car?'

'I didn't see it.'

'Clothes?'

'Just clothes. Jeans and a windcheater. They all wear jeans and windcheaters.' Hilaire spoke with contempt. 'And cowboy boots. He was wearing those.'

'Everybody west of the Iron Curtain wears cowboy boots these days,' Pel said dryly.

'It had been raining,' Hilaire went on. 'And the girl had a red plastic mackintosh on.'

'She still had it on when she was found. It's the man I'm interested in.'

'He – yes, of course – ' Hilaire's expression became excited ' – he wore a beard – '

'They all do nowadays.'

' – and he had a birthmark on his face. About here.' Hilaire's hand touched his cheek just alongside his ear.

'Nose? Eyebrows? Jaw?'

'Just a nose. Not much in the way of eyebrows. Jaw – you couldn't see it for the hair. He didn't look the sort of guy I'd want my daughter to marry.'

'Why not?'

'He was scruffy. I bet when he did his military service he was the bane of his sergeant's life. I bet he spent all his time dodging duty and avoiding keeping himself clean.'

Pel frowned. Hilaire seemed to have Le Bihan's habit of making up backgrounds for people.

'He talked too loudly, too,' Hilaire was saying. 'And he laughed too much.'

'On drugs, would you say?'

'I don't know people on drugs.' Looking at Hilaire's hard honest face, Pel could well believe it. 'But he might have been.'

'Smoke?'

Pel was thinking of cannabis but it turned out to be Marlboro, because the bearded man had bought a packet from Hilaire. All the same, the description seemed to make sense. Perhaps Dominique Pigny had lived with the man, thrown him over and tried to start a new life and they were quarrelling because of it. Pel stopped dead. Name of God, it was infectious. First Le Bihan, then Hilaire. Now *he* was at it.

They were silent as they drove back to the city. Pel's mind was working swiftly. Where had Dominique Pigny come from? It was unlikely that she came from Mongy because in a place of that size Bardolle or Hilaire, both of whom seemed to have sharp eyes, would have spotted her before – and undoubtedly have found out her history.

So, if she didn't come from Mongy, where *did* she come from? Had she come in her companion's car, if he had one? Or had they just met in Hilaire's bar? Had she a car of her own? And if not, how had she reached Mongy? By bicycle? On foot? Had she had a lift? And if so, with whom?

When they reached the Hôtel de Police it was late in the afternoon and as they pushed the door open the policeman on the desk looked up.

'Someone in your office, Patron,' he said. 'Someone to see you.'

To Pel's surprise, sitting in his office was Didier Darras, looking uneasy and scared. Alongside him was a girl whom Pel assumed was Louise Bray. She was very young, barely into her teens, but she was slim and pretty and he found himself admiring the boy's taste, but wondering nevertheless what had brought them. He'd got to know Didier well. He'd lightened many an hour when Madame Routy had weighed heavily on Pel's shoulders, but, apart from expressing the ambition to be a policeman himself, he'd never asked to see the police at work.

'Hello,' Pel said. 'What are you doing here? Did you enjoy the caves?'

'No, sir.' Didier jumped to his feet, surprisingly formal. 'This is Louise. I've told you about her.'

The girl managed a nervous smile. There was something about them that indicated anxiety and Pel wondered what it was all about. Had they been indulging in sex together and was the girl in the family way? It was far from impossible these days. He frowned, wondering if they'd come to him for advice, and decided it called for a cigarette.

He waved to Didier to sit down, then taking out the cigarette, lit it slowly to give himself time to think. Shaking out the match and placing it carefully in the ash tray, he turned towards them. 'You in trouble?' he asked.

They glanced at each other then Didier spoke. 'I don't think so,' he said.

'Then what – ?'

Didier sat up stiffly. 'It was this afternoon – '

'At Drax?'

'Yes.'

'In the caves?'

'Yes.'

'Did something happen?'

'Yes.'

Pel paused. 'Well, go on,' he prompted. 'What?'

Didier looked again at the girl, then swallowed. 'We found a body,' he said. 'A dead body.'

seven

For a long time Pel was silent. After the initial reference to the ticket found on Dominique Pigny which indicated she'd been to the caves at Drax, he'd thought no more about the place. Now, suddenly, he began to wonder if there was a connection between her and this new body Didier had found.

'Inform me,' he said.

Didier cleared his throat. 'The main part of the caves,' he said, 'is easy to get into. But you have to pay, so we tried another part about a kilometre further on. You can get in for nothing there. It's shallow, hard to get into, full of rocks, and no good to potholers because it doesn't go far down, so nobody ever goes there.'

Pel studied the boy, aware of how fond he had become of him over the years. The idea of him landing into danger worried him.

'I had a torch,' Didier went on.

'I imagine you'd need one,' Pel said dryly.

'Yes, sir.' The boy was still surprisingly formal, not at all like the boy who argued with Pel over Scrabble and helped infuriate Madame Routy. More like a witness on a witness stand, in fact.

The two of them were drinking Coca-Colas from the Bar Transvaal, both nervous and inclined to eye each other as if to draw confidence from each other's presence. Cadet Martin, who had fetched the Coca-Colas, sat at the desk with his notebook. Nosjean – brought in because, since with

Hilaire's evidence, they appeared to have a murder on their hands already and it might be necessary for him to take over this new one – leaned on a set of files.

Didier cleared his throat again. 'She – '

'She?'

'It was a woman. She was under a slab of rock – '

'Under a slab of rock? Buried?'

'Sort of.'

'Then how did you manage to find her?'

'I moved the rock.'

'Why?'

'Why?' Didier seemed startled at the question.

'Yes, why did you move it? One doesn't go around moving large slabs of rocks in underground caves for nothing. Especially if they're big, and I imagine this *was* big if it was extensive enough to cover a dead woman.'

Didier hesitated and looked at the girl.

'Well, actually,' he said, 'there were *two* – large and flat like slate – overlapping each other. The piece I moved wasn't all that heavy.'

'Why did you move it? You haven't explained why?'

Didier blushed. 'We'd been fooling about,' he said. 'Louise was scared of spiders and things and when I saw this big slab, I thought it probably had some more under it and that she'd grab me again.'

'She grabbed you when she was frightened?'

'Yes.' Didier managed a ghost of his old grin. 'I liked it. I put my arms round her to calm her.'

The girl blushed and he continued. 'When I saw this slab I thought she'd be particularly scared, so I could have my arms round her for a long time. I – ' he swallowed ' – but when I lifted it I saw this foot. It looked old-fashioned.'

'It was horrible,' the girl said.

'She'd been dead a long time,' Didier went on earnestly. 'I'd often wondered what it would be like to see a dead body but this one had been dead so long it wasn't as bad as I'd expected.'

'How do you know it had been dead a long time?'

'Just that it was all – well, sort of – well, thin. Shrivelled.'

'Starved?'

'No. Just old.'

Pel looked at Darcy. This was unexpected. The appearance of a body in the caves at Drax hadn't startled him because of Dominique Pigny's interest in the place but the discovery of an *old* body was a different matter entirely.

'It was flattened,' Didier was explaining. 'Brown. It looked ancient. I didn't see the face. I put the slab back.'

'Did you see anything else?'

'I didn't look.'

Pel's voice grew sharper. 'I thought it was your ambition to be a policeman.'

'It is.'

'Then start behaving like one. You must have seen more than that.'

'Yes, sir.' Didier sat up and his manner became brisk. 'I saw a handbag.'

'Near the body?'

'Yes, sir. That was flat, too. Sort of squashed. The rock, I suppose.'

'This body: How do you suppose it got there?'

Didier swallowed. 'I reckon it was put there, sir. The rocks couldn't have killed her by falling on her because she'd have had to be lying down for that to happen. I don't think they were heavy enough anyway.'

'Good. Good. You're using your brains now. Did the body look as though it had been placed there recently?'

'It had been dead a long time.'

'It could still have been placed there recently. Do you think it had?'

'No, sir. There was mould on the shoe. And little marks in the earth – the sort that mice make – going underneath it.'

'This is better,' Pel was being deliberately enthusiastic and it was working well. The scared looks were going. 'Then, if the body had been there for a long time, why do you think it hadn't been noticed before?'

Didier gestured. 'You couldn't see it. And nobody would have moved the slab. There were other smaller stones piled on top of it.'

'Which you moved in the hope of finding spiders?'

'I – ' Didier blushed again ' – I was showing off a bit.'

'It's a failing males have in the company of attractive females,' Pel said and this time it was the girl who blushed. 'So you moved these other stones?'

'They'd been there a long time. You could tell by the moss. It had grown from one to the other across the gaps. I began tossing them aside and then I saw these two long flat ones. I said something about it being the grave of a missing heir of Philip the Bold and that they'd have surrounded it with treasure like the Egyptians did with their kings. Then – then – ' Didier's voice, which had begun to rise as he described the excitement of the pretended search, fell again abruptly ' – then I lifted the slab. There was a slot between two rocks and I saw this foot. That's all. We stared at it for a bit.'

'I didn't scream,' the girl said.

'Good,' Pel said. 'Very good.'

'No,' Didier agreed. 'We didn't panic. I put the slab back just as I found it. I remembered what you'd said about being a detective. We didn't touch anything. I just lowered it, that's all. Then we came out and got on our bikes.'

'Why didn't you report it to the police at Drax?'

Didier shrugged. 'I thought you'd know what to do better than some brigadier at Drax.'

Pel nodded, touched that the boy had so much confidence in him. He paused and stubbed out his cigarette. 'Well,' he said, 'this raises a point. Are you prepared to take me back and show me exactly where this body is?'

'No,' the girl said at once.

'I hardly expected that,' Pel admitted. 'I'll have you taken home. In a police car. By Cadet Martin here. How's that?'

The girl looked at Martin. He was a good-looking youngster and the idea obviously appealed. 'Yes,' she said. 'I think I'd like to go home.'

'And you, Didier? Are you prepared to go with me and show me the spot?'

'Yes, I'll go.'

As the girl disappeared with Martin, Nosjean straightened up. 'I'll lay everything on, Patron,' he said. 'Photography. The Lab. Doc Minet. We'll need lights, and I'll telephone Drax to expect us.'

As he left, Didier turned to Pel. 'I'll show you where it is,' he offered. 'But if it's all the same to you, I'll stay outside.'

'Policemen need to have strong stomachs, mon brave.'

'Yes.' Didier's smile was more like the old smile now. 'But, I think I'll wait until I'm a policeman.'

It was dark when they arrived, but the Drax substation was waiting eagerly. Drax was a quiet place like Mongy and the policemen had the air of men who had waited all their lives for this very moment to show what they could do. The brigadier's wife was looking after the telephone and every man had turned out and was waiting by the little cream Renault van they used.

The caves were situated in a flat face of rock like a cliff just above the road to Langres. It was holed here and there as if by giant rabbits and at one end there was a group of huts – the pay booth, the refreshment booth and the gift and postcard shop – all closed until the tourist season got going in July. The owner of the land looked bewildered.

'They telephoned that there was a body in one of my caves,' he complained.

The entrance Didier had found was on the high land above the road and to reach it they had to turn into a winding lane that curled up the hill to where there were steeply sloping fields, broken here and there with clumps of rocks and steep little valleys. There were more of the holes here but these were small and, in the dark, it was difficult to find the one Didier had entered.

As they finally stopped at the entrance the farmer started complaining again. 'I've never seen a body in there,' he said.

'How long is it since you were in there?' Pel asked.

'I don't think I've ever been in this one, to tell you the truth. The land here's like a rabbit warren.'

As they gathered by a narrow fissure between two rocks, Didier touched Pel's arm. 'I'd better come in with you,' he offered.

Pel put a hand on his shoulder. 'You don't have to.'

'I don't mind.' Didier's mouth was firm. 'It's all right with you here.'

'A boy in a small moment becomes a man,' Pel said sagely. 'Very well. Lead the way, Nosjean. I'll bring up the rear.'

It was difficult to squeeze through the fissure but inside they found themselves in a cave as wide and long as a tennis court. The roof was low and the walls were streaked with green and yellow.

'Over here.' Didier led the way across the uneven floor and, in a smaller cave like a side chapel in a church, they saw the scattered rocks he had moved. He pointed to the far end of the cave.

By the wall there were two long flat slabs of slatey stone which, as the boy had said, looked like a broken coffin lid.

Nosjean and Pel leaned over them, studying them carefully for anything that might be of help, then Pel nodded.

'Up with it, mon brave,' he said.

Placing his lamp on the floor, Nosjean reached for the slab. There was little to see but the brown flattened foot Didier had described. The body appeared to be covered by a large sack and only the foot and a leg protruded where it had rotted away. As Didier had said, beneath it small marks showed the tunnelling of tiny animals.

Cautiously, Pel reached for the top of the sack. It was pulled away easily and, immediately, he saw a round object covered with a mould and a crushed straw hat with wilting artificial flowers, surprisingly unfaded despite the time which had obviously elapsed since it had been placed there. The round object was a skull with the remains of a human face still discernible, even a small well-shaped ear, on which a few strands of reddish hair were coiled. Beneath they could see nostrils, an open mouth, teeth, empty eye sockets and brown mummified flesh.

Flattened by the weight of the stones the body reminded Pel vaguely of the corpse of a rabbit flattened on the N7.

He looked up at Nosjean. 'It's some time since this was put here, mon brave,' he said slowly. 'I think this will be one for the historians.'

eight

Long after Didier had been taken home, they were still at the caves.

They had to move very carefully. The sack covering the body had come away easily, showing clothing beneath which was also friable and easily torn, but the skin of the corpse had proved rock hard and the limbs were stiff enough to resist any attempt to move them.

When Photography, Leguyader of the Forensic Laboratory and Doc Minet had finished, a spade, borrowed from the owner of the caves, had been used to lever the body from its niche. It had remained as rigid as if made of concrete, crouched, its head twisted to one side; the skin of the face was brown, the remainder of the corpse a lighter yellow, the shape of the body, hips, buttocks and breasts of a woman quite discernible. The skin was marked here and there with holes made by maggots but the ears were shapely and the teeth were all present. The eyebrows, eyelashes and hair, apart from the one small coil over the upper ear, were missing.

It wasn't easy removing it from the cave because of the narrow entrance, but the body was hard enough and stiff enough for them to manoeuvre it in its plastic sack through the opening and lay it on a stretcher, before carrying it to the van which shot off, its headlights glaring in the darkness, towards the forensic laboratory.

Watching it go and the policemen still laying out tapes, erecting lamps and taking measurements, Pel was puzzled. Not only did they have to find out who the dead woman was and how she came to be where she was, they also had to find out why Dominique Pigny had been to the caves. What had seemed at first to be merely a casual visit now seemed to assume some importance.

Coron, the owner of the caves, could offer little light on the subject and he had no memory of any visitors around Ascension Day who might have been Dominique Pigny, who in any case wouldn't have visited the cave where the mummified body had been found.

'Any of the visitors show any special interest in their surroundings?' Pel asked.

'Just the usual "oohs" and "ahs". We have special lighting effects. There's one grotto we call the Virgin Mary's Grotto. There's a stalagmite that looks a bit like the Virgin and child. Actually, we chipped a bit off to make it look better but we keep that to ourselves.'

'Can you think of any reason *why* anyone should be specially interested in these caves?'

'They're good caves. But there's nothing you can steal except the floodlighting. And that would require a pantechnicon and a gang of electricians.'

Pel rubbed his nose and sniffed. 'Remember a girl in a red plastic mackintosh?' he asked.

Coron shrugged. 'Red plastic mackintoshes are popular these days.'

'Did anyone ask any unusual questions?'

'Not that I remember. No, hang on a minute, there *was* something. Mostly they stand about looking like fish in a goldfish bowl and you wonder if they're even interested, but this girl – well, she wasn't really a girl any more – she asked if anybody had ever lost their way in the caves. I told her we were too well organised. Then she asked if anyone ever had in the past and if any bodies had ever been found. I said we didn't go in for bodies. And I've been in most of the caves at times to store things or take shelter in a rainstorm.'

'Do they usually ask if bodies have ever been found?'

'Not usually. But this one did and she was very insistent. Went on and on about it.'

'Which,' Pel said thoughtfully, almost to himself, 'seems to indicate that when Dominique Pigny came here she already knew of that body we found, but not where it was. What about potholers?'

'We get a few. Just amateurs and kids. The caves don't go down far enough.'

'Any of them ever report anything strange?'

'Such as what?'

Pel's eyes glowed. 'Such as someone caught stuffing a body in a cave.'

Leguyader, of the Forensic Lab, looked cheerfully at Pel, certain that this time they had come up with a beauty.

'How long has she been there?' he said. 'Twenty-five years. Perhaps thirty. Perhaps even forty. At the moment, I can't say.'

He looked at Pel as if he had achieved a minor triumph. He was a small man, as bad-tempered as Pel himself and given to undue sarcasm and, because he didn't like Pel – since it was mutual, it didn't worry Pel overmuch – it was always his pleasure to present him with problems that couldn't he solved. After a lapse of so many years, he felt certain this one couldn't.

He sat at the other side of Pel's desk with Doc Minet, smugly pleased with himself. 'Those caves are dry and well ventilated,' he went on, and Claudie Darel, who had just produced coffee for them, paused at the door to listen.

Doc Minet moved in his chair. Unlike Leguyader, he loved his fellow men so that he and Leguyader made a strange combination.

'She's not strictly a mummy,' he said. 'Though mummification's certainly taken place. It would appear it was a natural process. There was free access of air and a gradual process of drying must have occurred. She's really just a shell of dried skin and bones because the usual process of putrefaction had taken place and with it the deposit of flies' eggs which eventually hatched and became larvae that devoured most of the soft tissues.'

Pel frowned. 'How long before we can have anything that might identify her?'

Leguyader and Minet exchanged glances.

'We've placed her in a glycerine bath,' Leguyader said. 'It'll take several days for the skin to soften enough for an examination. At the moment, it's impossible to move the limbs or alter the position of the head, which is twisted as if she had a wry neck. Have we anyone who disappeared who suffered from a wry neck?' Leguyader rubbed his hands cheerfully, content that the facts so far were so nebulous as to be almost valueless.

'There's nothing else?' Pel asked.

'No. When the years have done their work the flesh disappears.' Leguyader was at his most pontifical. 'And after mummification takes place it's very difficult to be certain of anything. I would say it's virtually impossible to state exactly when she was placed there.'

Pel sat in silence for a moment. Was she a war victim? Probably as long ago as forty years, Leguyader thought, which meant death *might* have occurred during the war. The university had been helpful, both about the geological effects of the caves on a body and about the incidents that might well have occurred there forty years before. Assuming the body had been placed in the cave at that time, as Leguyader suspected, then it had happened at a point in history when France had been occupied by an enemy. Thousands of

Frenchmen had been living away from their homes, and there were thousands of Germans around, probably even Americans, Poles, English, and God knows what. Was this one a foreigner? Pel frowned. He could see it was going to be a tough one.

When he presented the report, the Chief was particularly interested because he had lived near Drax as a boy.

'But I never heard of any fatalities in that area,' he admitted. 'Though people used the bigger caves for air raid shelters when the bombers came over. Could she have gone in, perhaps in terror, and hurt herself? Fainted, perhaps, and died?'

'It's hardly likely,' Pel said. 'She was wrapped in a sack with stones on top. Besides, there are no records of any bombs falling in that area. Goron was there as a boy throughout the war and he doesn't remember any. And she couldn't have been flung into the spot where she was found. It wasn't possible.'

Pel was still intrigued by Dominique Pigny's interest in the caves. Had she known about the body? Was she searching for it? Had she heard of some old crime and gone investigating? It sounded the sort of crazy thing she might have done. But if she *did* know, *how* did she know? And why would she know of a body which had been in the caves without being discovered for years before she was even born?

It was quite obvious they weren't going to make much headway until they'd established the identity of the dead woman and the intelligent thing to do was to bring the press in on it. At Pel's summons, they arrived outside his office like a pack of hounds in full cry. Fiabon, of *France Dimanche,* Sarrazin, the freelance, and Henriot of *Le Bien Public.*

Giving them the details, he left it to them and the following day, half of France was aware of the corpse in the caves of Drax.

'WHO IS SHE?' *France Soir* demanded. 'HOW DID SHE GET THERE?'

'CAVE FIND HORROR,' *France Dimanche* said, producing pictures of Didier and Louise Bray.

'BODY FOUND IN CAVE.' *Le Bien Public* was always more conservative than the others.

That weekend sightseers turned up at Drax in such droves Coron decided his season should start earlier than normal and in no time the pay booth and the souvenir shop were open. Unfortunately, nobody was interested in the main caves with their coloured stalagmites and stalactites, concealed lighting and the statue of the Madonna, while the cave where the body had been found had been roped off and two policemen occupied the entrance.

'Nobody goes in there,' Pel had ordered.

The policemen had looked at each other. Drax was a long way from anywhere. 'How long are we likely to be here, Patron?'

'Until you're relieved.' Pel couldn't resist sarcasm. 'There's a tap near the pay booth so you'll be all right. Water's always more important for survival than food.'

nine

With Pel occupied with two murder cases – one of their own and one which still belonged to Le Bihan by virtue of the fact that the body had been discovered in Beg Meil – it was difficult for Darcy to do more than make arrangements that he should be constantly watched. With the Chief's permission, he arranged that Aimedieu and Morell should take turns to cover him at all times, then he set about the almost impossible task of searching Montchapet where Philippe Duche had last been seen.

Montchapet was a spiderweb of streets, all of them old enough to be narrow but none of them old enough to be a curiosity. They'd been built around the period of Napoleon III and time hadn't improved them. There were a lot of bars and Darcy moved quietly from one to another until he learned that a man answering to Duche's description had been seen in an apartment in the Rue de Lomy.

The apartment was as cramped as a rathole, with the walls patched with damp and the stink of urine and stale food on the stairs. The furniture was shabby, the settee held upright with a house brick in place of a leg. The owner was a man called Sacha Guinot, known to his associates as The Russian. He was small, unshaven, with the blank vicious eyes of a ferret, and had been in and out of 72, Rue d'Auxerre, which was the name by which the local prison was known, most of his life. He'd been brought before the magistrates on charges of assault, fraud, burglary, carrying an offensive weapon, beating his wife – who had left him as soon as she'd seen him safely sent down the line – conspiracy, cruelty to children, robbery and even attempted rape. He was well known at the Hôtel de Police and Darcy saw no point in beating about the bush.

'I'm looking for Philippe Duche,' he said.

Guinot's small evil eyes blinked. 'What have I to do with Philippe Duche?'

Darcy smiled. 'He used to be a friend of yours.'

'I wouldn't give him house room.'

Darcy's voice grew harder. 'You *did* give him house room,' he snapped. 'Last week.'

Guinot's face fell. 'It's a lie!'

'No, my friend. It's no lie. He was seen. You weren't careful enough. Had he a gun?'

'No.'

'Give him one?'

'Where would I get a gun?'

'*Did* you give him a gun?'

'No.'

'Sure?'

'You can trust me.'

Darcy's smile came again, showing his strong white teeth.

'I'd trust you, my friend,' he said, 'about as far as I could throw a grand piano. Where is he now?'

'I don't know.'

'You can do better than that. Has he got a girl?'

Guinot shrugged. 'He had one.'

'Who?'

'Name of Marie-Celeste Brionne. They call her Carmen Cocu because she was on the streets for a while. She probably still is.'

'Where's she live?'

'She had a flat in the Rambollet district.'

'Address?'

'Rue Lamartine. Flat 4, Number 5.'

Darcy closed his notebook. 'Good. Keep your nose clean.'

Guinot shifted uneasily. 'With you bastards around I've got no option.'

Always preferring to know his subject, Darcy headed back to the Hôtel de Police and looked up Marie-Celeste Brionne, alias Carmen Cocu. She was a Marseillaise by birth and had a record for soliciting, shoplifting and carrying an offensive weapon – to wit, a knife – with the intent of doing grievous bodily harm to another girl who had elected to frequent her pitch.

Armed with the knowledge, Darcy drove to Rambollet, and knocked on the door of Flat 4, Number 5, Rue Lamartine. It was opened at once and Marie-Celeste Brionne appeared with a smile on her face, which vanished at once as she saw Darcy.

'You a flic?'

Darcy flipped his identity card at her and studied her. 'Expecting someone?'

'Just a friend.'

She was small, dark and surprisingly pretty, but somehow she seemed to go with Philippe Duche because her eyes were cold and her voice was thin and hard. She was wearing a housecoat with not very much underneath.

'Wouldn't be Philippe Duche, would it?' Darcy asked.

She gave him stare for stare. 'Who's Philippe Duche?'

'You know who Philippe Duche is. Has he been here?'

'I haven't seen him for two years. I've got better things to do than get mixed up with men like him.'

'Stop lying.' Darcy thrust his way inside the flat and stared around. There was no sign of Philippe Duche's presence, until, as he pushed the door to, he saw a pair of men's shoes tucked away in the shadows behind.

'Whose are those?' he asked.

She shrugged. 'My father's.'

'Your father's in Marseilles. I've checked.'

'He's been on a visit. He left them by mistake.'

Darcy gave her a push and she sat down heavily on the settee.

'Philippe Duche has a foot about that size,' he said. He was still moving through the flat, his eyes everywhere. In the bathroom, he picked up a safety razor. The blade was covered with short stubbly bristle.

'Yours?'

'I shave my legs.'

Darcy looked down at them. 'You're dark-haired. Why is the hair on the razor blond?'

'My friend must have used it. She was staying with me.'

'You're a liar,' Darcy said. 'But, unfortunately, not a good one. This is chin stubble. I think I'd better take you in.'

She looked nervous. 'What'll happen to me?'

Darcy was casual. 'A month or two inside. Philippe Duche's an escaped prisoner, and he's wanted.'

'He's nothing to do with me.'

'He is if you hide him. You could be in the dock with him.'

She looked scared now. 'All right, I'll tell you. He was here. But he only stayed one night.'

'One night. Two nights. A month. A year. It makes no difference. You'd better come clean. Where is he?'

'He left the city.'

'Marseilles? Paris? Somewhere like that?'

'I don't think so. He said he'd be back. I don't think he's far away.'

With a car, you could be within reach of a city fifty miles away. And a circle drawn round the city fifty miles from its centre covered a lot of ground. Darcy looked at the girl. Despite her hard calculating eyes, there was something pathetic about her youth.

'You're wasting your time with Philippe Duche,' he said.

'He wants to marry me,' she snapped defiantly.

Darcy shrugged. 'Philippe Duche would never marry you. You haven't the class. Philippe Duche thinks he's big time. He chooses girls without records. He's like his brother.' Darcy paused, wondering how much good the lecture would do. 'And he'll end up like his brother, too. Dead.'

Six days later Doc Minet and Leguyader, of the Lab, appeared in Pel's office with the results of their examination. After five days in a glycerine bath the skin of the body found at Drax had softened sufficiently for an examination to be made. As they had straightened it out the twisted neck had fallen into a normal position.

'They're the remains of a European woman between twenty and forty,' Minet said, accepting a cup of coffee from Claudie Darel. 'But it's not possible to establish the age with any certainty. The bones on the right side were better developed than those on the left, which suggests she was probably right-handed. Apart from fragments, the internal organs have disappeared due to the action of fly larvae but we decided she was not pregnant at the time of her death.'

Pel leaned forward and Claudie paused by the door to listen as Doc Minet continued.

'There appear to be no injuries to the skull and the strange position of the head was due to the way she'd been crammed into the slot in the rocks where she was found. There were no fractures of the chest. A softening fluid of ethyl alcohol, formalin and sodium carbonate was used on her and chemical tests indicate no poisonous substance was present.'

'We found animal bones in the cave,' Leguyader said. 'Which is understandable because it could have been a fox's lair, but there was nothing to indicate the possibility of a violent death there. She was dead when she was placed there.'

'What about identification?'

'The teeth are all there,' Minet said. 'But dental records weren't kept as immaculately in those days as they are now, and, since it was probably wartime, a lot of things were allowed to lapse.'

'Because of the weight of the stone on her,' Leguyader went on, enlarging on their theme, 'everything about her became married into the flesh. The sacking, the clothing, the stockings. It's even possible to see the marks of a fold of the sacking along what remains of the cheek and even the hem of the dress has left a mark along the outer thigh.'

Leguyader was clearly set to talk all day and Pel interrupted quickly. 'How did she die?' he asked. 'I can read the details in the report.'

Leguyader sniffed, affronted. 'We seem suddenly to have discovered the importance of our new position,' he said.

Pel glared. His feud with Leguyader was a long-standing one. Leguyader glared back and Doc Minet hurriedly came to the rescue to avoid trouble.

'She was strangled,' he said.

Pel swung in his chair to face him. 'Can you be certain?'

'Absolutely. The upper horn of the thyroid cartilage was fractured. It's a little bone and it never gets broken alone, except when the neck's gripped tight by a strangling hand. It's the pressure of a finger tip or thumb that does it.'

'Could it have been fractured during a fall? Could she by the wildest chance have been flung down by the blast of a bomb and injured her voice box against a stone? And then, perhaps because of bad weather, have crept into the cave for warmth and died there? Perhaps even found the sacking already there and wrapped it round her against the cold?'

'And covered herself with stones?' Leguyader said coldly.

Pel ignored him and looked at Minet, who shrugged.

'It's not impossible,' he said. 'It's even possible that her body was later found by someone who thought he ought to give her a decent burial and placed her in the crevasse and covered her with the stones. But not the broken bone. I've seen the whole thyroid crushed, with fractures of both horns and both wings. I've also seen one wing and one horn broken together. But never only the horn, and I've examined hundreds of cases. The only time I've seen it has been in cases of manual strangulation. Besides – ' as he paused, Pel leaned forward again ' – on the material of the sack we found a yellow deposit which, when analysed, was found to be the remains of slaked lime. Whoever placed her there probably used it to keep down the smell of decomposition. Perhaps, even, it was hoped to destroy the body because lime has a reputation for destroying flesh. But if that was the reason, whoever used it had his facts wrong. Slaked lime has no destructive action. In fact, it would kill insects, which would cause it to act as a preservative. It's because of the lime that there were fragments of the internal organs still remaining so that it was possible to guess she wasn't pregnant, and it also helped to preserve the injuries to the throat.'

'Go on.'

'We calculated the height when alive at around a hundred and sixty centimetres with a centimetre or two either side. At the maximum, a hundred and sixty-five. At the minimum a hundred and fifty-five.'

'Age?'

'It's hard to tell.' Minet gave a little smile. 'And I don't think you need be in a hurry. Whoever put her there will have stopped running long since. Still – ' he shrugged ' – to give you an idea: I think she was young. In her twenties. The teeth were good and well formed. Slightly built. Reddish hair – '

'Well, there's less of that around than there is of the other colours.'

'It was done in plaits coiled round the ears. I think they were called "earphones" in those days. Hands – as far as we can tell, in good condition, as if she didn't do manual work.

Even perhaps not much housework. She was married. Or at least on her left hand was a wedding ring – not a very expensive one. But no engagement ring, which is odd because most married women usually wear both, though the engagement ring, being the more valuable, is worn on the outside so it can be removed when washing or doing housework. She also wore no earrings but her ears had been pierced and the holes seemed to have been torn, as if the earrings might have been removed in a hurry.'

'As if she'd been killed for her jewellery? A straightforward robbery with violence?'

Minet shrugged. 'Shoes,' he went on. 'In good condition. Slight. Neatly built. Probably careful of her appearance.'

They discussed the possibility for a long time and when Leguyader and Minet had gone, Claudie Darel put her head round the door. 'That body, Patron,' she said. 'Perhaps I could help.'

'You have experience of pathology?' Pel asked.

'No, Patron,' Claudie said calmly. 'But I have a lot of experience of being a woman, and I probably know more about fashion than Doc Minet.' She gestured at the photographs Leguyader had left. 'I could check the clothes at the library to get a rough date. It might save a lot of time. I imagine quite a lot of girls have gone missing in the last forty odd years.'

'The most recent,' Pel pointed out dryly, 'at Beg Meil a month ago. And by a curious coincidence she'd been to Drax, too.'

The autopsy on the new body was held in the ante-room of the council chamber where Pel had recently been entertained by the Chief and, since the real work had already been done, it was merely a formality with almost the same dignitaries present as at Pel's party. They talked about everything but the corpse, then climbed into cars to visit the scene of the crime.

They then retired to the hotel at Drax for lunch, and there was a lot of handshaking and hat raising before they finally disappeared, satisfied that duty had been done.

When Pel returned to his office, feeling remarkably mellow considering the task they'd been performing, he found Claudie Darel had already made progress.

'I think she died around 1944,' she said.

'Which is what Doc Minet and Leguyader thought,' Pel pointed out.

'I'm *sure*, Patron. Her shoes have wooden soles and that places it firmly during the war. Well-dressed women have never worn wooden soles on their shoes except during the Occupation.'

Pel studied the girl quietly. She was clearly bursting with excitement. 'There's more, I can tell.'

'Yes, Patron. The fact that she died during the Occupation makes it harder to pinpoint what class she belonged to, because things were difficult to obtain and everybody wore what they could get hold of. But I think she was different from most women.'

'In what way?'

'The handbag's of good quality, and the hat had style. I think she was someone who was fashion-conscious. There were two shades of lipstick in her handbag, together with eye shadow, something which wasn't much used in those days. In fact, she was carrying quite an array of cosmetics so she was probably keen on her appearance. It therefore follows that she was probably pretty.'

Pel sat quietly, listening

'I'm checking the hat,' Claudie went on. 'It looks as if came from a Paris milliner's, though there's so much copying done it could well have been copied locally from a picture. The shoes had labels which indicate they were bought in Paris. Which seems to suggest she moved around a bit, even though she spent some of her time here. Actually the clothing looks almost modern because those fashions are all the rage again now but none of it's man-made fibres, and that dates it at once. Besides, the underclothes – ' she smiled ' – they just aren't modern underclothes. They're of satin. Nowadays they'd be of nylon. And they're not brief enough. Nowadays women don't wear very much underneath. I'd like to find someone who knew her.'

'Try Madame Caous,' Pel said. 'She might well have bought her clothes at the same shops.'

Making a note of the name, Claudie looked up again. 'I think there was something special about her, Patron,' she said. 'The earphone style of hairdressing was out of fashion with young women forty years ago. So I'm wondering if she kept her hair long for a specific purpose.'

Pel looked at her shrewdly. She was using her brains.

'If she were a model for instance. Perhaps she modelled hair styles. Or else she appeared in front of people. As a performer.' Claudie smiled. 'I think, Patron,' she ended, 'that we wouldn't be far out if we looked for a red-haired actress.'

ten

So now they had two females, one unidentified, both young and attractive, and both violently dead, but surely unconnected because there was almost half a century separating their deaths.

The following morning, they took another step forward in the Pigny case when Bardolle telephoned to say he'd found the man with the cherry marking on his face.

'Gérard Crussol,' he said. 'That's his name. There I was asking questions all over Villiers-sur-Orche. And it turned out to be Villiers-St-Rémy, which is about fifty kilometres from here. North-west of Châtillon.'

'North-west?' The words came to Pel's mind at once. Hadn't Madame Charnier thought her sister, Dominique la Panique, had a boy friend somewhere 'in the north-west'? Obviously, when Dominique Pigny had mentioned him, she had been thinking of her base around Arne or wherever she'd been staying, so that 'north-west' had only been north-west of there and was hardly Brittany. But it was in the right direction.

'And how did you perform this miracle, Bardolle?' he asked.

'Not very difficult, sir,' Bardolle said. 'Had a stroke of luck. A few months back his car broke down. Petrol pump packed up and because they hadn't one in stock at the garage in Mongy he had to leave it for a day or two. They remembered the mark on his face and they were able to turn up his address. Aged thirty-five, divorced, lives alone. He's a stonemason and works for a funeral director called Chevallier in Châtillon.' Bardolle gave a huge laugh that almost shattered Pel's eardrums. 'No wonder he was so noisy in Norbert Hilaire's place that night. Working for an undertaker. All those stiffs. Having to be quiet and respectful all the time. If I had to keep quiet like that, I'd burst.'

Pel could well believe it. 'We'd better go and see this Crussol,' he said.

Because of the threat from Duche, Darcy was with Pel. There had been a break-in at a restaurant in Chemilly which was on the way, and money had been stolen. Not much, but a 6.35mm Star automatic, owned by the proprietor and fully licensed because of the need for him to keep large sums of money on the premises over the weekend, had also disappeared.

'Our friend, Duche, would have to get close to hit me with a 6.35,' Pel said.

'Don't be too sure, Patron,' Darcy retorted. 'A 6.35 will kill at ten metres but there's a case on record of a man being killed by one at eight hundred. Eighty per cent of the shootings in the States are with what we call 6.35s.'

Crussol's home looked like a stable, an ugly building with a shabby front garden that seemed to be littered with pieces of broken stone. The gates were of cheap tubular steel covered with what looked like sheep wire, and, like the rest of the building, had obviously recently been decorated in crude red and purple paint that seemed to have been chosen and applied by a colour-blind amateur; the colours shrieked their disagreement and the paint sprinkled the hedge and the trees, and there was a large lavender handprint on the wall.

Crussol was not at home so they retired to a bar on the other side of the road from which they could watch the house, and sat in the sun drinking beer as they waited. Pel always enjoyed the feel of the sun on his old bones. It was in his nature to consider himself advancing rapidly through the arches of the years and he had long been convinced that he hadn't much time left before they carted him off in a box to the cemetery.

Darcy's eyes were moving about them all the time, and Pel watched him, amused. 'Surely you don't expect to find Philippe Duche here?' he asked.

Darcy didn't smile. 'Where we find Philippe Duche,' he said, 'is where you are and where we won't expect him to be.'

They were still there as evening approached so they decided to eat a quick meal. The girl who served it had hair that seemed to have been fried in olive oil and so much mascara on her eyes she looked as if she were a miner fresh from the pit. The meal tasted of old shoelaces and the wine like anti-freeze.

'I often wonder,' Pel said, 'why police pensions don't take into account the damage done to police stomachs in the performance of duty.'

He lit a cigarette, and studied it gloomily. 'They say it dulls your sense of smell,' he muttered. 'If I stopped, they could probably put me on a lead and get rid of the sniffer dogs.'

Darcy grinned. 'I shouldn't worry, Patron,' he said. 'You've got a few non-smokers in your team now. Morell's one.' He looked pleased suddenly. 'He called me "Patron" the other day. I suppose now we ought to up you to "Patron of Patrons" or something. "All Highest," perhaps.' He looked warmly at his superior. He knew all Pel's little weaknesses and still admired him. 'You've come a long way, Patron.'

Pel nodded. 'The first time I put on uniform,' he said, 'I was so dim I didn't know my back from my front. They sent me out on the streets with a sous-brigadier to show me around but he had a girl friend and after half an hour he disappeared to see her, and I suddenly realised I didn't know where I was. I was terrified of having to arrest someone and having to ask him the way to headquarters.'

As he finished speaking, Darcy put his hand on his arm. A battered old Citroën was coming slowly up the street. The front had been pushed in by a collision and it had so much rust on it, it looked as though it had spent some time on the seabed. One of the tyres was almost flat and a headlight was missing. As it passed them, they saw the driver, a large man with the shoulders of an ox. He was bearded and they could distinctly see a cherry-coloured mark on his cheek.

'That's him,' Darcy said.

They watched him open the ugly gates, park the car in the concrete drive, then close the gates after him and disappear into the house. The door slammed so hard it seemed as if he were trying to pull the wall down on top of him.

They gave him plenty of time to get himself established then they rose, paid their bill and headed for the house. At their knock, the door was wrenched open and Crussol stared out at them, a huge shabby, hairy figure like a bear, his clothes covered with white dust and minute chippings of stone.

'What do you want?' he demanded. 'I'm working.'

'So are we,' Pel said. 'And we want a word with you.'

As he showed his identity card, Crussol stared at it blankly. 'Holy Mother of God,' he said slowly.

'You were expecting us maybe?' Darcy asked silkily.

'No.' Crussol grinned suddenly. 'It was just a surprise, that's all. I've not been involved with the police before.'

'Only when you were brought before the magistrates on an assault charge,' Pel pointed out.

Crussol's eyebrows came down and his fists clenched. 'That's a lie!'

'I don't think so.'

'Are you doubting my word?'

'It's our job to doubt what people expect us to believe.'

Crussol's expression changed and he shrugged. 'Well, it was worth a try,' he said cheerfully. 'How did you find out?'

'You have a file, my friend,' Darcy said.

'You mean they keep records of every little thing?'

'Assault's not all that little.'

'I was drunk. I don't go around getting into trouble.'

'How about a little matter of obtaining stone from a quarry at Chantenoy without paying for it?'

'That's nothing.'

'It was to the man who quarried it.'

Crussol gestured. 'I've got to have stone. I'm a sculptor.'

'Your record says you're a mason.'

'I work for a funeral director, that's all. Chevalliers', of Châtillon. To earn enough money to be a sculptor.'

'You've exhibited?' Pel asked.

Crussol scowled. 'I can't get anybody interested. The bastards who own galleries all seem to have minds like dwarfs. Things have to be pretty – birds and flowers and baby rabbits. Come in, come in.' He stepped back so they could enter. 'I'll show you what I'm working on. I'm not a criminal. I've nothing to be ashamed of. I bet you didn't find anything else in my file.'

'Only three or four "driving without due cares".'

'Well, I drive fast.'

'It shows,' Darcy said. 'On your car.'

Crussol laughed. 'My mind's often on other things. I have a tendency to wander about the road.'

As he held the door open, they saw that the interior of the house had been decorated in the same ghastly red and purple as the outside, the paint as liberally scattered on the floor and stairs as it was on the sidewalk and the hedge. The hall was small and seemed remarkable only for the amount of white dust everywhere and the stone chippings that were scattered about.

As Crussol opened another door they found themselves in the garage. In the centre of the concrete floor stood an enormous chunk of white stone, with what appeared to be two feet carved in one of the bottom corners. Crussol left them staring at it while he slopped beer into glasses from one of a number of bottles on a table by the wall.

'What is it?' Darcy asked.

'Jesus raising Lazarus from the dead.'

'What happened to Lazarus? He looks as if a house fell on him.'

Crussol gave a hoot of laughter. 'That's good,' he said. 'I must remember that.' He swallowed his beer in one huge draught. 'Have a drink,' he suggested. 'There's plenty. What can I do for you? I bet you didn't come to watch me at work.'

Pel fished out the photographs of Dominique Pigny from the brown envelope. 'I think you know this girl,' he said.

Crussol's glance at the photographs was casual. 'Sure,' he said. 'It's Dominique la Panique. What's wrong? Has something happened to her?'

'She's dead. Her body was recovered from the sea in Brittany fifteen days ago.'

Crussol hurriedly sloshed more beer in his glass. 'Poor old Panique,' he said. 'I wondered what had happened to her.'

'How well did you know her?'

'As well as you know someone you've lived with. She modelled for me for a bit. She wasn't much good. She wouldn't sit still and when she didn't want to do something she didn't. She could be tough. But she had a good body. Nice tits. Well-shaped feet. I like feet.'

'Where were you on the night of the 16th of last month?'

'In the bar across the road, I suppose. That's where I usually am in the evening. You can ask them. They'll have noticed me. People do when I'm in a bar.'

'Was she with you?'

'No. I was on my own.'

'You *were* with her in a bar about a month ago. In Mongy. The Bar Giorgiou. You had a meal.'

Crussol nodded. 'That's right. It cost me a fortune. She could always eat. They didn't have much on the menu so she had two helpings. Big ones. It always amazed me where she put it because she wasn't all that big. I felt a bit responsible for her.'

'Why?'

'We met at art school. She was studying art, too. But she wasn't much good at it. Most of them aren't and most of them never earn a living at it.'

'Do you?'

'Yes. As a mason.' Crussol paused and went on slowly. 'She could never handle feet, and feet are important. You can get away with hands. Shove 'em in pockets. Stick 'em behind backs. But you can't disguise feet, and most people get them looking like waders.' He paused, his eyes distant. 'We were younger then and life seemed hard for people of our age. It does sometimes. We got on to drugs. Me first. Then old Panic. Fortunately, we got off them again quick and I don't think it did either of us a lot of harm. Certainly not La Panique. She went in for jogging instead. She had the constitution of a wild horse and about as much sense. Just when she was at her most affectionate, she'd disappear for weeks at a time. In the end it got me down and I got this job in Châtillon. Carving gravestones and headpieces. Crosses. Weeping angels. Broken columns. That sort of thing. People haven't got much imagination. You should see the cemeteries in Italy. There's one in Genoa with a tomb of black marble shaped like a coffin with the lid open and a white marble hand hanging out. Limp. Dead. As if the corpse had tried to escape and failed. Superb. All we go for here is cherubs and angels and that sort of thing. Still – ' he smiled and gestured with his glass ' – cherubs and angels have feet. I also get my stone cheap. It's not bad stuff either. A bit like

English Hoptonwood. And the money's all right, and I pick up a bit extra now and then because they get me to give a hand with funerals. Carrying the coffin. Only they can never find anyone the same size and, with me at one end, the coffin's always up-ended and when you're carrying it with your head up close you can hear the stiff sliding down inside.'

'Dominique Pigny,' Pel prompted, feeling they were drifting off the subject a little. 'What was she like?'

Crussol shrugged. 'Good type. Warm-hearted. Full of life. Always good for a laugh. She became a fitness fanatic, did you know? After the dope jag. Walked everywhere. Round shops. In parks. In fields. On the hills. She exhausted me. Name of God, you aren't given feet for walking. You get them to press accelerator pedals.'

'So why this meal you had together?'

'She asked for it. I think she was in need of money.'

'What for? To go to Brittany, for instance?'

Crussol pulled a face. 'It would be like her. She was a bit mad – '

'Mad?'

'Spooky. You know: She did weird things and she didn't have many ethics. She wouldn't have recognised an ethic if she'd met one on the stairs.' Crussol scratched his head. It dislodged a small fragment of stone that fell into his beer. He studied it for a second, took a deep drink and poured what was left on the floor. 'I decided I was beginning to do all right,' he went on. 'My mother died a year ago and left me this place. Old Panique never seemed to stay anywhere for long but I thought she was beginning to fancy a bit of security and I was fond of her in a way. You know how it is. Perhaps I was getting broody. I agreed to meet her.'

'How did she get to Mongy? Had she transport?'

'She could drive, I know, because once last year she turned up in her sister's husband's car. She didn't tell her sister and there was a hell of a row. But I didn't see her with a car at Mongy so I assumed she'd come on the bus.'

Pel produced the photographs of the Lucie necklet. 'Ever seen that before?' he asked.

'Is it valuable?'

'Yes. It was found on her body.'

'If you think *I* gave it to her, you have to be joking. I couldn't afford a set of plastic beads.' Crussol grinned. 'My women have to take me as I am, without the additions of jewellery, jet flights to Florida, a château on the Loire and a summer home at St. Trop'.'

'Was she wearing it when you saw her?'

'If she had been, I'd probably have asked her to pawn it and lend me the proceeds.'

'Did she seem happy?'

'We had a smashing evening.'

'The proprietor thought you were quarrelling.'

Crussol laughed. 'That was nothing. We were always throwing things at each other. She was a dead shot. Once hit me on the head with a saucepan from across the kitchen. Iron one. Knocked me cold.'

'What was the quarrel about?'

'Me. I asked her to marry me.' Crussol gestured. 'I need someone to look after me. I never seem to get around to that sort of thing myself. I get absorbed in what I'm doing and forget to eat. It's obvious. You've only got to look around. It was only a working arrangement I was thinking of, but I'd done the place up. Inside and out. I got the paint cheap from a garage. It's for car bodies actually, and it'll peel in time, but it looks all right, don't you think? She didn't think much of the idea.'

'Was there someone else?'

'Yes.'

'Did she say who?'

'No. But there was a type she knew called Pineau – Paul Pineau. I thought it might be him.'

'Know where he lives?'

'No. But the girl she shared a flat with in Besançon might.'

'Name?'

Crussol grinned. 'Name of God, you are inquisitive, you lot. Déon or Léon. Héon, that was it. Odette Héon.'

'Did you know she was pregnant?'

Crussol's eyes lifted. 'Oh, no,' he said. 'Poor old Panique!'

'Was it you?'

'No. We never – well, hardly ever. She was always keen, you see, and I seduce easily. But it was a long time ago. Over a year. I hadn't seen her since until we met at Mongy.'

It seemed that Dominique Pigny had made the arrangement to meet by telephone.

'For a change I'd paid the bill,' Crussol said. 'And it wasn't cut off.'

She had had money and her clothes had looked good. Normally she wore jeans but on this occasion she'd been wearing what looked like an expensive dress for a change. Crussol had no idea where she had telephoned from or where she was living.

'She wouldn't tell me,' he said. 'She just said she'd got a job.'

'What was it? What did she do?'

Crussol shrugged. 'All sorts of things. She got into university but dropped out after a year. Then she did some modelling for me. She didn't like it much, though. I work from the heart and I just set up the stone and let fly. And when I'm at work you could fire a howitzer in my ear. She didn't like being made to look square either. "Head, neck, tits, bum," she used to say. "Always a square block." But if you see things as squares that's how you have to cut 'em up, isn't it? Then she used to complain that I didn't give her enough rests. Perhaps I didn't – I forget when I'm busy – and she used to howl that her leg had gone dead. In the end she threw a hammer at me.' He gestured at the window. There was a broken pane. 'I'll have to put that in one of these days.'

There was a long pause before Pel spoke again. 'What about your wife?' he asked.

'She left me. She didn't like square tits either.' Crussol sighed. 'It was a mistake from the beginning. She had hands like coal grabs and when she took her clothes off, she had feet like flippers.'

'Where is she now?'

'Haven't the foggiest. She threw the soup at me one evening and walked out of the door. I've never seen her since. I heard she'd set up house with a type in Limoges, but I don't know.'

'Did she know about Dominique Pigny?'

'She'd gone long before Dominique moved in. I suppose it was my fault she left. I used to insist on her stripping off and sitting for me but in those days we couldn't afford any heating so like old Panic she always ended up blue with cold. I used to have to uncoil her when she took a rest, she was so frozen. I ought to have noticed, I suppose, but you can't spend all your time looking at the model to see if she's all right, can you? They always *seem* all right until they fall off the chair in a dead faint. I suppose women aren't as strong as men. She said she couldn't go on. I suppose she couldn't. She wasn't very bright but she was a good looker and not bad in bed.'

There was another pause. 'Have you ever been to Drax?' Pel asked.

'That place where there are those caves?'

'That's right.'

'They found a body there, didn't they? A million years old.'

'Yes. Ever been there?'

'No.'

'How about Dominique Pigny? Had she?'

'How would I know?'

'Did she ever mention them?'

'No.'

'What happened after she left you?'

'She worked in a shop. Selling clothes. For this Pineau type. Then she disappeared for a bit and took a shorthand and typing course. But she never worked at it. She decided she didn't like office work. Then she tried a hospital, but she said everybody being ill made her miserable. She also worked in a bookshop. Once for a time she got a job looking after horses somewhere. But it didn't suit. She was a bit of a drifter really. I thought if we got married, it would stop. But – ' Crussol sighed ' – perhaps it wouldn't. I expect I'd have made her unhappy. I usually seem to.'

'Are *you* unhappy?' Darcy asked. He spoke briskly, because Darcy had probably never been unhappy in his life. If anyone was master of his fate and captain of his soul Darcy was.

Crussol studied him as if he realised it. It was hard not to, because it shone out of Darcy's spotless shirt and immaculate suit, out of his closely-shaven chin and neatly-cut hair and the strong white teeth that showed every time he smiled.

'Sure I'm happy,' he said. 'Give me a block of stone and a chisel and I'm as happy as a kid on its pot.'

'Think he did it, Patron?' Darcy asked as they drove homewards.

Pel shrugged. 'We'll let Le Bihan sort that one out,' he said. 'It still seems to be his case.'

When they reached the office, Claudie appeared. She had edged forward another notch.

'I've found a woman whose mother made hats here during the war,' she said. 'She lives in Tournus. I've arranged to see her tomorrow. For a time she ran a shop here for a Paris firm that had premises all over the country. They went bust during the war when material became hard to get, and she got married and stayed at home to look after her family. But, because she didn't know what to do with them, she kept all the records. She's still got the customer list in the cellar and she's going to dig it out for me. It might take a day or two. She's not as young as she was.'

'A lot of people aren't as young as they were,' Pel said, thinking of Madame Caous and the ancient corpse they'd found at Drax. 'In fact, we seem to be knee-deep in geriatrics.'

eleven

Two days later, Le Bihan arrived in Pel's office, his vast bulk looking like a badly set jelly in the heat.

'Thought I'd like to see this Crussol type,' he said. 'I might be able to break him down a bit. Want to come along?'

'It's your case,' Pel pointed out.

He took Le Bihan to lunch at the Central where Le Bihan, as Pel – with one eye on his expenses sheet – had feared, ate enough for three, before being sent on to Villiers with Aimedieu as guide and counsellor.

De Troquereau was still pursuing his enquiry into Madame Boyer's missing ducks. Pel didn't interfere. Like Nosjean, De Troq' was one of Pel's favourites and, because he was a baron, Pel liked to announce him, when they were working together, by his title rather than his rank. It made Pel sound like the head of the Sûreté.

He had read all he could about ducks, and about Indian Runners in particular, and bearing it all in mind, had concentrated on egg producers instead of farmers who bred for the table. Finding one called Lucien Gautherot at Louisvillers, who had twenty-four Indian Runners among his flock, he was intrigued to notice his farm was only twenty-five kilometres from Cholley, where the ducks had vanished.

'Where did you get them?' De Troq' asked.

Gautherot was a fat man with a florid face and most of his meals down his waistcoat. 'Bought them in the market at Rimbeau,' he said. 'Month ago. Might have been five weeks.'

'Pay by cheque?'

'In a market?'

'Know the type you bought them from?'

'Never seen him before.'

'Where did *he* get them?'

'He said he bred them.'

'Get his name?'

'Why should I want his name?' Gautherot was friendly enough but there was a sly too-clever look about him that De Troq' didn't trust.

Returning to Cholley, he found Madame Boyer feeding the chickens and what remained of her ducks.

'If you saw your ducks again,' he asked her, 'could you identify them?'

'Easily.'

'Well, I've found some at Louisvillers. How about coming with me and telling me if they're yours?'

Madame Boyer looked at the huge open car with its vast headlights, standing behind De Troq'.

'In that?'

'Why not?'

She stared at him, then her face creased into a vast smile. 'Just let me get my coat.'

When she reappeared, she'd put on lipstick and her best dress and coat, and had a handkerchief tied round her head to hold her hair in place. She was obviously regarding it as an afternoon out with the aristocracy.

'Mind going fast?' De Troq' asked.

'Not likely.' She very nearly said 'With you, I'd have a go at anything.'

But, her hair blown by the slipstream and her cheeks whipped to pink by the blast, as they looked at the ducks over the wall of Gautherot's farm, her face fell.

'They're Indian Runners,' she said. 'But Indian Runners all look the same. Like Indian Runners. I dare bet they're mine but how can I be certain? They don't answer to a name.'

About the time Madame Boyer was looking at the ducks in Gautherot's field, Claudie Darel was taking tea with Madame Caous. The former manageress of the hat shop had produced nothing. The mice had used her records to make nests.

Madame Caous was delighted to see Claudie, who was presented with afternoon tea and cucumber sandwiches. 'A la Grande Bretagne,' Madame Caous pointed out. 'They say that the Princess of Wales has them every day.'

'So exciting,' she went on as she pottered with the crockery. 'Two police officials in so short a time. Though I'd never have dreamed you were a detective. You're so pretty. I do hope that when you meet a criminal you'll be sure to call one of your male colleagues.' She patted Claudie's arm. 'I used to be pretty, too. Men used to run after me. Do they run after you?'

'From time to time,' Claudie said, thinking of Nosjean and De Troq'.

Madame Caous listened carefully to her requests but she looked a little puzzled. 'Is this the same unfortunate that Chief Inspector Pel came to see me about?'

'No, Madame. A different one.' Claudie explained about the body at Drax. 'We're hoping we can find who she is so her relatives can claim her.'

'Perhaps they won't want to,' Madame Caous said. 'Perhaps, after all this time, they've lost interest. People do, you know. When they came to bury Voltaire, they found his heart was missing and it was supposed to have been mislaid in a desk drawer and sold to a junkman.'

She dug deeply into her memory. She could remember no names, but she could recall a girl disappearing some time during the war.

'I seem to remember reading about it on my birthday,' she said. 'I was born on Ste. Sophie's Day. May 25th. We're so lucky in France. We have a saint for every single day, don't we? And plenty of extra all-purpose ones no one has ever heard of that the Church can call on when they're needed, such as St. Blaise for tonsillitis. I'm sure you'd find what you're looking for if you look through the local paper about that time. I remember it said she'd probably been done away with because she had a large and expensive engagement ring on her finger. It was a diamond and I remember it because a policeman I knew – he used to come into the shop to see me and used to pretend he was checking up on things, but I think he was just checking up on me – he told me it had a stone in it big enough to choke a horse. Those were his words.'

Claudie frowned. 'She wasn't wearing it when she was found,' she said. 'Is he still living in this area?'

'Oh, mon Dieu, he might have gone to meet his Maker long since! He was a very handsome young man.'

'Do you remember his name?'

Madame Caous smiled. 'I remember the names of all my admirers, my dear,' she said. 'Especially the good-looking ones. It was Marcel Bardu.'

Aimedieu returned in the evening after putting Le Bihan on the train to Paris, where he would have to change for Concarneau. 'He can certainly drink, that one, Patron,' he said. 'He'll sleep all the way to Paris and when he wakes up the inside of his mouth will feel as if it's grown hair.'

'Did he decide Crussol was the killer?'

'No. just the opposite. But he could have been. That type's got a temper.'

'Did he throw something at you, mon brave?' Pel asked mildly. 'He often does, I believe.'

Aimedieu looked like a choirboy as he blushed. 'Not at me, Patron. At the wall. His hammer. A heavy round stone thing. It had knocked a lot of plaster out. He was working on a thing called – '

'Jesus raising Lazarus from the dead.'

'It looked more as if a safe had fallen on him from a second floor window and he was trying to lift it off.'

'Squares,' Pel said. 'He believes in squares. What happened?'

'He'd chipped off a toe he hadn't meant to chip off. When we arrived he was still trying to decide whether to hack out a fresh foot, make the ones he'd got a bit smaller or give them four toes like Disney characters.'

While they were talking, Claudie Darel appeared. Her eyes were shining and her cheeks were pink with excitement.

'I've found her, Patron,' she announced at once. 'Her name was Joséphine Cellino, known professionally as Josée Celine. She was an actress. Your Madame Caous was more useful than she realised.'

She explained what had been said then went on excitedly. 'I went to Records but there was a gap of several years that I couldn't understand until I found that a bomb had destroyed them.'

'So?'

'So I went back to the newspaper and dug out their files for May and June during that period of the war. And there it was: May, 1944. Josée Celine, aged twenty-three. Red-haired – red-haired, Patron! – and an actress. Somebody concerned with her appearance, someone who'd wear fashionable clothes. Last seen at Dismagnay near Drax, on or about the 14th of May. She was fairly well known and appeared in one or two plays – but nothing of importance – and a lot of musicals outside Paris. I think she was just a glorified chorus girl but she must have been clever – or shrewd – because she'd done well and when she disappeared she was supposed to be wearing an engagement ring with a diamond on it big enough to make her walk lopsided. "Big enough to choke a horse" was the phrase the police used at the time.'

'She wasn't wearing it when she was found,' Pel pointed out. 'And how did she get it? Chorus girls don't have engagement rings of that calibre. She must have had a wealthy admirer.'

'She did. She'd been living with a type called Xavier Sirdey. He was a wealthy engineer who had a house at Dismagnay. He was suspected of murdering her and disposing of the body.'

'It looks very much as if he did. Go on.'

'He claimed she left him. The whole district was searched and large areas were dug up, but nothing was found and it was impossible without the body to prove anything. She'd been through a form of marriage with this Sirdey but her relatives were suspicious and after she disappeared they found he'd already got a wife. He was charged with bigamy, which was the best that could be done but, without Josée Celine or any form of document, the case fell through. After that the thing seems to have been gradually forgotten and by the end of the year it had dropped out of the news completely.'

That evening Pel met Madame Faivre-Perret at the Relais St. Armand. Though Madame didn't know it, Aimedieu was sitting in a police car just outside. It seemed a pity to Pel because the Relais St. Armand was where he and Madame had originally met and it held as much romantic appeal as anything could for someone as unromantic as Pel. However, with Claudie's news about Josée Celine, his mind was far away and he barely heard what Madame was saying until she brought up the subject of housekeepers, at which point he sat bolt upright and began to take notice.

'I've been thinking,' she was saying, happily making plans as they ate. 'Above my office at the hairdressing salon there are rooms which would make an excellent apartment. It's in the centre of the city and we could make it comfortable and interesting.'

After his house in the Rue Martin-de-Noinville, the office over Madame's business had *always* been interesting to Pel. He'd often suffered fantasies, as he was shown upstairs to her office, that he was mounting to his mistress' bedroom.

But three homes! Name of God, if he weren't careful, he'd be a plutocrat!

'It would be a wonderful place to use when you're busy,' Madame said. 'Being over the business premises, it would always be aired and, when you were working late, it would save you having to go all the way out to Hauteville. I could simply move in and look after you.'

Oh, wonderful woman, Pel thought. What had he done to deserve such devotion?

'Won't it be a lot to look after?' he asked uncertainly.

Madame's mouth moved in a small smile. 'We can have a housekeeper for Hauteville.'

Pel blanched. 'A housekeeper?'

'When I've finished a day's work, I don't feel like doing very much. And I'm sure you don't.'

Pel was silent. After Madame Routy, the last thing he wanted was a housekeeper. He'd been thinking of Madame herself cooking his meals, pressing his clothes, putting out his slippers, being in his bed.

A housekeeper! He decided it needed the application of a certain amount of low cunning. However, he felt he knew quite a bit about low cunning. Most of his days were spent countering the activities of criminals *noted* for their low cunning, and because his own cunning was lower than theirs most of them ended in the jail at 72, Rue d'Auxonne. He decided he could work something out, given time.

Taking Madame home – Aimedieu following discreetly behind – he set off down the hill towards the Rue Martin-de-Noinville. As he reached the Porte Guillaume, he turned off towards the railway station and the Hôtel de Police. He couldn't bear going home without making sure the place was still functioning smoothly.

Darcy was still in his office, sitting by the telephone.

'Found Duche yet?' Pel asked cheerfully.

Darcy didn't regard it as a joke. 'Did *you* see him tonight, Patron?' he asked.

Pel's eyebrows rose. 'Should I have?'

'A man answering his description was seen in a car near the Relais St. Armand while you were eating there.'

Pel frowned. He was beginning to be irritated by the threat of Philippe Duche. 'Who saw him?'

'One of Nadauld's uniformed boys off duty. He followed him in his car but lost him in the traffic.'

'Nadauld's boys would lose their right arms if they weren't screwed on.'

'It's no joke, Patron.'

'I didn't imagine it was, Daniel. What do you propose to do?'

'I'm switching Aimedieu to the search. From now on I'm sticking alongside you. Especially as Nadauld's man thought he headed north out of the city.'

'But I'm *here,* Daniel. *In* the city.'

'At the moment, Patron. But you're going *out*. North.'

'I am?'

'I've had Bardolle on the telephone again. He's got an old boy out at Mongy he thinks we ought to see.' He consulted a notebook. 'Name of Gaston Jourjon. Known as Le Gaston.

Does the ditching and hedging for the farmers whose fields border the Violette-Mongy-Mercourt road. He's been doing it all his life. He hasn't a television and doesn't buy newspapers but has them given by neighbours after they've finished with them, and he's just seen the picture of Dominique Pigny that appeared a week ago. He told Bardolle he saw her walking into Mongy two days before she was fished out of the sea at Beg Meil.'

Pel's eyebrows shot up. 'Then if he saw her two days before she was found she must have decided to go to Beg Meil immediately afterwards.'

'Unless she went unwillingly. This Jourjon says that when she passed him there was a car waiting up the road in a lay-by that had been waiting there on and off for three days. If what he says is true and there *was* a car there, perhaps it was waiting for *her.* And if that's so, she probably wasn't killed in Beg Meil but here. In which event, it's not Beg Meil's case. It's *ours.*'

twelve

When they arrived at Mongy the following morning, Bardolle was waiting for them.

'Le Gaston's ready,' he said.

Pel looked about him. 'Where is he?'

'At work. He wouldn't stop. I don't think he knows how to. He's been at it all his life. Same thing, day after day, month after month, year after year.'

'Couldn't you bring him in?'

'I'd have to club him, Patron.' Bardolle levered his huge bulk into Darcy's car and sank into the rear seat. The car immediately took on a heavy list to starboard. 'I'll direct you. It's a lovely morning. It should be nice out there.' It was clearly Bardolle's enjoyment of his little diocese that made him such a happy man.

'Who is this Le Gaston anyway?'

Bardolle shrugged his enormous shoulders. 'Well, he's a bit of a liar, but you can't ignore what he's got to say because of that. And he's well known round here for not minding his own business.'

'What's that mean?'

'He's a voyeur. Uses his job to creep about fields and watch youngsters romping in the grass.'

Le Gaston was busy at the side of the road. He was a small strong-looking old man with a face wrinkled by a thousand suns. His trousers were tied up with string and his cap sat at an unbelievable angle on the side of his head. Long before they were within hailing distance they could see his head bobbing up and down in the ditch. He had cleared the weeds and laid them in little piles along the side of the road and, further along, one of them was smouldering. He was now trimming the hedge, using a billhook to cut half-through the branches so he could bend them over and weave them round stakes he was hacking from the woods behind.

'Every five years,' he said. 'It needs this treatment every five years. They get neglected.'

'They prefer to pull 'em up these days,' Bardolle pointed out bluntly. 'They reckon a few large fields are easier to cultivate than a lot of little ones.'

'No good for cattle,' Le Gaston said. 'They waste the grass. Besides, hedges cut the wind. Stop soil erosion. And when they go, the wildlife's lost.'

Pel made his presence known with a cough. Le Gaston looked up, but he didn't seem to think much of Pel and he didn't stop.

'They want to know about that girl,' Bardolle said. 'The one you told me about.'

Le Gaston gestured with his billhook. It almost removed Pel's nose. 'I saw her,' he said. 'Passed me on the road here, Walking. Good walker. Nice legs, too. Strong.' He gave a little cackle. 'And I never saw such a behind. Nor such a before, come to that.'

'Where had she come from?'

The old man pointed. 'Up yonder. Only place she could come from.'

'What's up there?' Pel asked.

'Leads through Arne,' Bardolle said. 'To Les Charmielles and Violette then back on to the main road.'

'Hiker?'

'She wasn't no hiker,' Le Gaston said. 'I seen her before.'

His head was still down in the ditch, his arms going like a wasp's wings, and Pel spoke plaintively. 'Think he could manage to stop for a bit? I don't enjoy talking to his backside.'

Bardolle fished in his back pocket and withdrew a flask. 'They'll usually stop for this,' he said.

Le Gaston was no exception. He climbed out of the ditch, laid down his tools, took the proffered flask and had a good swig.

'You say you saw her before,' Pel said. 'Where?'

'Here. I live here. In Mongy. They won't mend my roof and it's leaking.'

'Never mind your roof, you old ratbag.' Bardolle said. 'When you saw her before, which way was she going?'

'Both ways. I saw her come down the hill and once I saw her go up.'

'So she must have come from somewhere on this road and was going back when she went the other way. Where would she be going the day you saw her?'

'Mongy or Mercourt. It was the 15th of the month. I worked it out. I was down there alongside the wood. I take a fortnight to get to here from the curve down there. Always have. For twenty years. *Musta* been the 15th.'

Pel looked quickly at Darcy. 'Six or seven days before she was fished out of the sea,' he said. 'And they reckoned she'd been in it for about that time. So she must have been walking down this road between twenty-four and thirty-six hours before she died.'

'I seen a car too,' Le Gaston said. 'Up yonder. Parked.' He took another swig at Bardolle's flask. Bardolle hurriedly took it back, and picking up his tools again, Le Gaston gave them a gap-toothed grin. 'Can't let me tools get cold,' he explained.

'What sort of car?' Pel asked as the old man climbed into the ditch again.

Le Gaston's head shook violently. Surprisingly, it didn't dislodge the cap resting over his left ear, which remained as firmly fixed as if it had been nailed there. 'I don't know no names of cars. Just a car. Will they mend my roof?'

'*I* wouldn't,' Bardolle said. 'Not if I were your landlord. Listen, what colour was this car?'

'White. Cream. That sort of colour.'

'What was it doing?'

'Just standing?'

'Get the number?'

The old man cackled. 'I can't see things like that. But I see it more than once. Just standing. Near the big house. I seen it three days runnin'.'

'Have you seen it since?'

'It never came back after the last time I saw the girl.'

'Anybody in this car?' Darcy asked.

'Man.'

'Did he see you?'

'Nobody sees me. I arrive as soon as it's light and when I go, everybody's already home. I'd go earlier if I had somewhere decent. Only my roof leaks.'

Bardolle frowned. 'Listen, you old lunatic. Did you get us out here just to draw attention to your roof? I wouldn't put it past you.'

As the interrogation limped along, Le Gaston offered little in the way of description. He had seen the girl and then, as it passed him, the car with a man in it and that was all.

'When did it pass you?'

'Soon after the girl passed me. She'd gone round the corner there when it came down.'

'Did you see what happened?'

'No.'

'Did you hear anything?'

'Brakes. I reckon he had to brake to miss her.'

'Or because he hit her,' Pel said. 'What you heard was probably the tyres. What time was this?'

'Late afternoon. Five. About that. I was in shadow.' The old man looked up at the sun. 'This time of the year the sun's over the hill there. I was packing up. Cleaning my hook. Putting it in a sack. Police are fair fussy about wrapping 'em up. Say the kids might harm themselves.' He gave a little cackle. 'Any kid that comes round my faghook deserves all he gets. You could shave with it. Cut a man's throat as easy as look at him. I wouldn't mind cutting the throat of the type who won't mend my roof.'

By the afternoon, a description of the car had gone out to all stations and substations for enquiries to be made at local garages, and Bardolle's men were making enquiries in the villages to the north while Lagé, Misset and Morell were working round Arne, Les Charmielles and Violette. Nobody had seen the girl, but Bardolle turned up a woman who'd almost been knocked down by a speeding car at the end of the afternoon of the 15th as she crossed the main street of Mercourt just beyond Mongy and to the north of where Le Gaston had been working.

'I had to jump for my life,' she said.

She hadn't got the number and didn't know what sort of car it was but it was white and she thought it was the same as the local doctor drove. They discovered the local doctor drove a Mercedes.

Suddenly they were making a little progress and messages were put out to all forces and all garages and repair shops at the car they were looking for was a Mercedes that had been brought in on or around the 15th, 16th or 17th of the previous month requiring repairs consistent with it having hit someone.

In the meantime, Pel contacted Inspector Le Bihan to inform him that it looked very much as though the case was about to pass out of his hands.

'Well, you're welcome to it,' Le Bihan said. 'We're certainly not getting very far here.'

However, he had one interesting item of news. One of the wealthy residents of Benodet, the next residential area to the west from Beg Meil, had reported a white car hanging about on the road that ran along the coast on the 16th of the month. She'd noticed it first because her small son was having a party that day and she'd thought it was the caterer bringing the food. She hadn't known the make of the car but her small son had: It was a Mercedes.

'It stayed until after dark,' Le Bihan said. 'There was a man in it. Dark. Sunglasses. Light-coloured suit, blue shirt. She thought he was nervous or a burglar studying the house. It stayed there most of the day and only disappeared at lunchtime. It wasn't there the next day.'

That night a dentist from Lyons called Bastien telephoned to say that he'd heard of the police interest in a white Mercedes and would they perhaps be interested in his? He gave its number and said it had been stolen on the 12th of the previous month, which was just before Dominique Pigny had disappeared and immediately before a white Mercedes had turned up in the lay-by on the road from Arne. It was, he considered, about time he got it back.

The number went out and under the circumstances, with Dominique Pigny fixed more firmly in their diocese, it seemed a good idea to see Madame Charnier's husband, who appeared to be the one person who might have a motive for murder.

Taking the view that, faced with his formidable wife, Charnier might be inclined to be reticent, they decided he would be better interviewed at his work. He was employed by a small manufacturer of agricultural implements and appeared in the dusty waiting room wearing an overall which seemed to swamp him but somehow seemed to go with his personality, as if he'd been swamped all his life by something or other.

He was a thin man with glasses and the look of a frightened hamster. Quite clearly, he had been dominated by the women in his life. His mother originally, without doubt, now his wife, and, at some point, her sister.

'I've never owned a white Mercedes,' he said. 'But I wouldn't mind. It might stop my wife going on about the old Peugeot I run.'

'Do you ever go to Benodet or Beg Meil in Brittany?' Pel asked.

'I've never been there in my life,' Charnier said. 'My wife's always going on about it. You'd think it was paradise. She used to live in Brittany and go there as a girl for August and she thinks *we* should.'

'You knew Dominique Pigny, I believe.'

'She was my sister-in-law. She's dead. It was in the paper.'

'She was pregnant. Was the child yours?'

Charnier seemed uncertain how to answer and Pel decided it might easily have been.

'You slept with her, didn't you?' he said.

'Who told you?'

'Your wife.'

'She would.' Charnier shrugged. 'Well, yes, I did. But it was her fault, not mine. She was always going on about it. Saying I was ineffectual. My wife did a bit, too, and one day I sort of went mad and thought I'd show them I wasn't.'

'Did you kill her?'

Charnier gave a bleat of protest. 'No, I didn't! There were times when I felt I'd like to, mind. She was a troublemaker if ever there was one. Always coming to my home and stirring it up. All the same – ' his eyes suddenly became far away ' – I've never regretted it.'

'Why?'

Charnier shrugged. 'Well, you know – '

'No, I don't know. Inform me.'

'Well, my wife – well, she and I – there was nothing to it. No grand passion. She just let me do what I wanted and never seemed to join in at all. She looked like Joan of Arc going to the stake.'

'And Dominique Pigny?'

'She was different.' For a brief moment, Charnier's eyes lit up. 'She believed in enjoying it. My wife seemed to think it was sinful or just for having kids, that sort of thing. Dominique said it should be fun and, name of God, she made it fun. They say you hear bells when you experience real passion. With my wife I didn't even hear a tinkle. With Dominique it was if all the bells in Notre Dame were going. My wife had gone to look after her aunt. The old witch was always going on about being ill and needing someone to look after her – that family were born troublemakers – and Dominique happened to be staying with us and said she'd look after me. Holy Mother of God, she did, too!'

'When was all this?'

'Over a year ago.'

'Then why did you hesitate when I asked if the baby was yours? Have you seen her since?'

Charnier hesitated. 'About three months ago. End of April, beginning of May. My wife was looking after her aunt again and I was looking after myself. She turned up on the doorstep grinning all over her face. "Sidonie's away, isn't she?" she said. I asked her how she knew and she said she'd telephoned her aunt who'd told her. She was on her way somewhere. Lyons, I think she said. She wanted somewhere to sleep.'

'Did she sleep with you?'

Charnier nodded. 'I didn't want to – or at least I did and I didn't – but I think it pleased her to do something like that to my wife. I think she thought it a good joke.'

'Have there been any other women?'

'One or two. With someone like my wife you have to get a little comfort where you can.'

'Did your wife find out about you and her sister on the second occasion?'

'I don't think so. But she might have. It would be just like Dominique to tell her.' Charnier's face changed suddenly. 'Does my wife know you're here?'

'No.'

'Don't tell her, for the love of God. It'll only all start all over again if you do.'

'I don't think there'll be any need for her to know,' Pel said stiffly. 'How did she regard her sister?'

'She didn't regard her at all. She just didn't like her.'

'Is that all?'

'Well, no. It was stronger than that. Because of – well, me and her. She was a great one for behaving yourself. She's the same with the kids. The whole family's the same. It was no wonder Dominique made a bolt for it.'

'Did she know about Dominique's baby?'

'She never said anything about it. But she might have found out.'

'If she did, she'd assume it was yours, wouldn't she?'

Charnier shrugged.

'She hit her sister on one occasion, didn't she?'

'She hit *me* on several.'

'Would you say she'd go to greater lengths than that? If she found you and her sister were lovers.'

Charnier hesitated and there was a gleam of malice in his eyes, as if he saw an opportunity to be rid of his domineering partner. 'Yes, I would say that,' he said. 'She hit Dominique with the broom. She knocked her unconscious. She might well have had another go.'

'*He* could have done it, Patron,' Darcy said as they started up the car. 'He doesn't look much like the type, but you never can tell. And if the baby was his, he had a good motive.'

Pel nodded. 'So had his wife. And if she could hit her sister hard enough to knock her unconscious, she'd probably be prepared to do more if she found them together again.'

'But *she* reported her missing, Patron.'

'The oldest dodge in the world to establish your innocence.'

'But how did she get her to Brittany?'

'They've got a car. And women have been known before now to hide bodies. Her husband probably wasn't unwilling to help her even. He's clearly short of money and wouldn't want to take on a baby. His wife could even have forced him, blackmailed him.'

'And what about the white Mercedes Jourjon says he saw?'

'Probably just a travelling salesman working the area who stopped in the lay-by to do his accounts.'

'And the one in Brittany?'

Pel shrugged. 'There are a lot of white Mercedes around,' he said.

thirteen

The following morning a report came in of a sports and arms shop in Dole being raided. Someone had removed iron bars at the back, climbed through a window and removed a Mannlicher 7mm hunting rifle.

Darcy climbed into his car and went with Aimedieu to have a look. The shop, with its sign 'Arquebusier, Pêche, Armes, Coutellerie,' was in the main street and for a second or two he stared through the window at the selection of fishing rods, knives, rifles and shotguns.

'Some gun-crazy kid,' the proprietor growled. 'He's probably out at this minute in the woods towards Rochefort looking for rabbits.'

'With a Mannlicher?' Darcy said. 'They know better than that, mon brave. He picked a German rifle because the Germans have a tradition for making the best. What else went?'

'Nothing. Just a telescopic sight. A Zeiss.'

'*Nothing*?' Darcy said. 'Just a Zeiss telescopic sight. That and a Mannlicher give him the world's best sniper's weapon there is.'

When Prélat, of Fingerprints, arrived, they went to work with the dusting powders. There was a large thumb print on the glass of the window where the intruder had entered and it didn't take them long to identify it.

Darcy looked at Prélat. 'Philippe Duche,' he said. 'This one isn't going to walk up to the Old Man's car and stick his arm through the window to pull the trigger. If he's got a rifle with a telescopic sight it means he's looking for a place where he can take a long shot.'

While Darcy was at Dole, De Troquereau was finally sorting out the case of the Indian Runners. At Cholley, he felt he was out on a limb, and he wanted to be involved in the case of Josée Celine – especially as Claudie Darel was involved, too. He had re-read everything he could find about Indian Runners and, finally deciding to try an idea he'd had, he returned to Boyer's farm and persuaded Madame Boyer to open wide the main gate and leave ajar the gate to the field where the ducks had been housed.

'What are you up to, mon brave?' she asked.

'I've had an idea. Just leave it to me.'

Packing into the back of his car two of the baskets with which she transported her ducks to market, he drove to Louisvillers. Gautherot regarded him smugly. He'd just had a meal and he was wiping his mouth with a red handkerchief.

'I want to borrow your ducks,' De Troq' said. 'For an experiment. There's a type over at Chizeux who has some like them and I'm a bit suspicious. You'd better get in your car and come, too.'

Gautherot was quite happy to oblige. It was quite clear he had no fears of De Troq' proving his ducks were Boyer's ducks. But as they passed the Boyers' farm and De Troq' drew to a stop, he pulled up alongside with an indignant look on his face.

'You said Chizeux,' he pointed out. 'This is Cholley.'

De Troq' shrugged and climbed out of his car. 'This'll do just as well,' he said.

Outside Boyer's farm, De Troq' checked that the gates were open, then, with Boyer and Gautherot watching, he got Madame Boyer to help him open the baskets. For a moment or two the ducks remained where they were, only their lean dark heads visible above the edge of the baskets, like a lot of elderly Indian ladies peering myopically about them. Then, one after the other, they hopped out into the roadway and for a moment longer they clustered together, before heading in a bunch for the gate to Boyer's farm. Quacking loudly, they vanished through the gate, across the yard and through the second gate, then, in a long line of tall brown waddling shapes moving at full speed, headed straight across the field to the shed where they'd been housed. One after the other they disappeared inside. De Troq' looked at his watch. It was seven-thirty.

'What time did you say you normally fasten up the ducks in their sheds?' he asked Madame Boyer.

'Seven-thirty,' she said.

Gautherot was standing by the car, his face red. 'I'll be over to see you,' De Troq' smiled.

Pel had just received De Troq's report when Claudie Darel appeared. She looked excited.

'We've confirmed her, Patron,' she said. 'Absolutely. Without doubt. She *is* Josée Celine, née Joséphine Cellino. Twenty-three years old. Born in Caen, Normandy. Green eyes. Red hair.' On Pel's desk she laid a photograph of a young woman, well-made-up and pretty, and wearing her hair in a style which looked modern yet obviously wasn't. Across the corner was a signature – 'Toujours, Josée.'

'Where did you get this?'

'Paris. Agence Barbanic. It's a theatrical agency. Books actors. They've got a collection of them and they say there might be more at the Musée des Théâtres.' Claudie laid a thick wad of paper on Pel's desk. 'It's all in the report, Patron. I've given a copy to Jean-Luc Nosjean. I've found the inspector who was involved in the original enquiries. He's still alive. He's seventy-five years old but apparently quite active. He lives at Talant. I'll go and see him.'

'Perhaps we'll *both* go and see him.'

'I've also found a friend of hers who toured the provinces with her. She's seventy-two years old – '

'Another one?'

'Another what, Patron?'

'We seem to be wandering down Memory Lane a little lately.'

Claudie smiled. 'She's got photographs taken during her theatrical career and Josée Celine's in a lot of them. She's digging out a selection for us because Grenier, of Photography, thought we might be able to compare them with photos of the skull from Drax. She remembers the rings she wore, too, and she says she *did* have a big diamond and she always wore earrings. Always. Big ones – as big, she said, as elephant's tears.'

'And Xavier Sirdey? What's known about him?'

Claudie smiled. 'He'd be around eighty-five years old, Patron.'

'Oh, name of God!' Pel extracted a cigarette from the packet in his drawer, trying to pretend it was a throat lozenge, but he'd hardly put it to his mouth when Claudie flicked a lighter and lit it for him. His bad habits, it seemed, were overtaking him.

'Well, if he's alive,' he said, 'he'll have to appear before the magistrates, despite his age. The law requires it. Have we any idea where he might be?'

'At the moment, no. He seems to have sunk without trace. I've contacted the substation at Dismagnay, and they've enquired. Only a few people remember the case, of course, and none of them knows where he went to. He seems to have left the district soon afterwards.'

Pel gestured. 'Very well. See Nosjean. We can't let it go. You and Nosjean had better stick with it. De Troq' can help, too. He's free now.'

She looked pleased because Nosjean and De Troq' were both young and good-looking and both were competing for her favours.

The Chief's interest remained casual. A body lost forty years before was hardly likely to stir the emotions much, especially since the man suspected of providing the body was more than likely also to be dead. The case of Dominique Pigny was different but Judge Polverari was still, despite the evidence of the waiting car, inclined to suspect a hit-and-run rather than a murder.

'The man in the car might have been watching the château,' he said. 'Some small housebreaker casing the joint.' He pointed to the map spread on the table between them. 'Where the car was parked must have placed the house well within view.'

Following the Chief's conference, Pel and Darcy made another journey to the Château d'Ivry. A small car was standing outside the main entrance when they arrived and they found a man inside talking to Bernadine Guichet.

'This is Doctor Lecomte,' she said. 'He's been to see Monsieur Stocklin. He thought he had a cold coming on.'

So did Pel. His throat hurt and he almost asked the doctor to give him a quick once-over.

Doctor Lecomte was a thickset man with heavy tweeds and a pipe as big as a lavatory bowl which poured out thick blue smoke.

'The old josser's all right,' he said cheerfully. 'Nothing much wrong with him except age.'

'He's old, doctor,' Bernadine Guichet pointed out.

'Name of Heaven, woman, these days people often live to be a hundred!'

He shook Pel's hand, crushing it in a vast fist like a coal grab. 'Police, eh?' he said. 'Who're you after? Old Stocklin? I expect the old rogue's done a few shady things in his time.'

'Any you've heard of?' Pel asked.

'Pure as the driven snow as far as I know. Priest says so, and he should know. I expect he's got all his sins down on a list, though, ready to send with him to Heaven when he goes.' Lecomte laughed. 'He's got a long wait, mind you. Barring accidents, he's safe for a century.'

Mademoiselle Guichet showed the doctor out and returned to offer tea to Pel and Darcy.

'I notice Monsieur Stocklin's window's on the north-west side of the house,' Pel observed as he polished off a biscuit. 'Overlooking the road down to Mongy. I was wondering if he ever saw the girl, Dominique Pigny, walking down it.'

'Why should he?'

'We have reason to believe she was on that road when she was killed. Perhaps he could identify the pictures of the girl we have.'

'I should doubt it,' Mademoiselle Guichet said. 'His eyes are too bad. But I'll go and see if he's awake.'

She slipped from the room and was gone for a few minutes before returning. Silently, she held the door open.

It was only a short walk along the corridor to Stocklin's room. The bed was huge, old-fashioned and heavily canopied and the room had the stifling atmosphere of age. It was nothing they could smell because there was a strong odour of antiseptic, clearly an addition by Bernadine Guichet, but there was a mustiness, a staleness, a lack of fresh air, as if it were the cage of an ageing eagle that was too rarely opened.

The old man was sitting on the edge of the bed in a dressing gown that had been fastened crookedly about him. He was thin and gaunt, with a long neck with a prominent adam's apple, his head covered with a fluff of white hair, and he was peering narrow-eyed at a television with a screen as big as a cinema, which was roaring away in a corner of the room.

Bernadine Guichet stalked across the room and turned it off. 'You should be resting,' she said. 'And there's someone to see you.'

The old man whirled and stared at Pel and Darcy. His face was yellowish, with deep lines from his nose to the corners of his mouth as if he'd never been in the habit of smiling much. He looked as if he'd always known what he was about and even now, despite his age, the faded eyes had a sharp look of cunning and malicious humour.

'Who's this?' he demanded. 'I didn't ask to see anyone. I never want to see anyone after that damned fool of a doctor's been.'

'You shouldn't be out of bed,' Mademoiselle Guichet said sharply.

'I'm not a cripple,' Stocklin growled. 'I could play football if I wanted to. With you, if I felt like it.'

'Not so much of that. Let's have you back where you belong.'

Slowly, she pushed him back into the bed. He stared at Pel and Darcy over her shoulder.

'Who *are* they?' he asked. 'Crooks? I don't like the look of them.'

'I'll tell you who they are when you're properly in bed.' She swung his legs in and covered him with blankets, the old man complaining all the time. Despite what she said, he seemed alert, though it was obvious from the way he peered at Pel that his eyes were bad.

'Well, come on,' he snapped. 'Who is it? He looks a bad 'un, that one.'

'This is Chief Inspector Pel, of the Police Judiciaire.'

The old man scowled. 'I don't like the police,' he said. 'Especially anyone called Pel. There was a man called Pel who cut up his wife in 1880 and burned her in the kitchen boiler. My father told me about her. What's he want?'

'He'd like to talk to you.'

'Well I wouldn't like to talk to him.' The old man gave a malicious chuckle. 'I don't think much of the police. They couldn't catch mice. What's he after?'

'He wondered if you could identify some photographs. Where are your reading glasses?'

The old man peered at the table alongside his bed. 'I had them a minute ago. They were here.' His hand groped among the objects on the table.

'You've lost them,' he snarled at Mademoiselle Guichet. 'With your everlasting tidying.'

The search ended with him cursing and thrashing about like a wounded whale under the blankets, and by the time they'd decided the spectacles had been lost the bed looked as though someone had played football across it.

'It's your fault,' Stocklin shouted at Mademoiselle Guichet. 'One day I shall probably shoot you.' He looked at Pel. 'I could,' he pointed out cheerfully. 'I've got a gun. She doesn't believe me because she doesn't know where it is. I keep it hidden. Together with my late wife's jewellery. I've got a secret place she doesn't know about because if she did she'd probably remove the jewellery for her own use.'

Bernadine Guichet looked at Pel and raised her eyes to the ceiling in despair.

'What's his memory like?' Pel asked quietly.

'Good, when he wants it to be. Abysmal when he isn't interested. Why?'

A thought had occurred to Pel and he leaned over the old man. 'Do you remember a murder case during the war?' he asked. 'An actress called Josée Celine.'

The old man's eyes flicked open and he stared at Pel. Then he nodded. 'Yes, I remember the case. I was near Vercors at the time.'

'Doing what?'

'I was with the Resistance. What else would I be doing in those days? She was a pretty little thing, I remember. I once saw her on the stage. She disappeared, didn't she?'

'They've just found her again.'

'They have?'

'She was living with a man called Xavier Sirdey.'

'Did he do it?'

'That's what we think. They couldn't pin it on him then because there was no body, and now there is *he's* disappeared.'

'Well, I don't know anything about him.' The old man cackled. 'But he was clever, that one. She was a bitch, I heard. Going round with other men. And the police were as stupid then as they are now. They never caught him. He laughed, I bet.' His face suddenly went blank and he heaved over in bed. 'I'm tired now. I want to go to sleep. Go away. I don't like policemen.'

As he subsided, still muttering, Pel put the photographs back in the brown envelope, uninspected.

'He wouldn't know her, anyway,' Mademoiselle Guichet said quietly as she led the way from the room. 'He's partly deaf and as you can tell he can't see very well.'

In her private quarters her brother had cleared away the tea things and was sitting at the table in a striped apron, cleaning a silver candelabra. As they entered, he rose and produced a bottle of marc.

'I've got a grandfather getting on for that age,' Darcy said as they drank. 'Thank God I don't have to see him often. Is he always like that?'

Guichet grinned and set about the candelabra again.

'Sometimes he's worse. He pretends a lot. He couldn't possibly remember the things he says he can.'

'Does he get out of bed?'

'He's not supposed to,' Mademoiselle Guichet said. 'But he does. You saw him.'

'Who looked after him before you?'

Mademoiselle Guichet shrugged. 'A variety of people. None of them stayed. He has too much of a temper. He's sly and shifty and pretends to be ill when he isn't. It makes it hard work. I keep thinking we'll have to have a change soon but the thought of him being on his own stops me. He'd have great difficulty finding anyone to look after him.'

'Has he no relatives?'

'None we know of. None *he* knows of.'

Pel studied the big rooms. 'Where did his money come from?'

It came from business but the Guichets didn't really know *what* business because Stocklin was no longer involved in it, though he still drew income from his land which amounted to around three thousand hectares. Everything round the house, including the farm and more land higher up the hill, to say nothing of a stretch of woodland looked after under contract by a garde forestier. There were also quarries at Chantenoy.

'They're very profitable,' Mademoiselle Guichet said. 'It's good stone. Undertakers use it a lot.'

Darcy stared about him. 'Don't you find it lonely here?' he asked.

Mademoiselle Guichet shrugged. 'You get used to it. I trained as a nurse. Then I left it for a time for another job, but as I grew older I didn't fancy what I was doing and I was just wondering what else I could do, when the man who'd employed my brother to look after him died and he had nowhere to go. So we thought of looking after old people together.' She paused. 'He's not fussy what he eats and he keeps himself amused. He watches television when he's not asleep. But old people are all the same and someone has to look after them. He's not the first we've had, of course. There've been several. When they're old it doesn't go on for long but it's not hard to find a job. When one dies there's always another.'

fourteen

It didn't take Darcy long to turn up Odette Héon, Dominique Pigny's former flat mate, in Besançon. It never did with Darcy and, organising Aimedieu, Lacocq and Morell to be within sight of Pel the whole time he was away, he took a day off that had been owed to him for a month, and made arrangements to talk to her in her lunch hour. She turned out to be tall with good legs and a jacked-up bust and he could hardly give her an Oscar for taste, because her flowered dress looked like a herbaceous border and Darcy liked his women svelte and sleek. But she had plenty of other attributes so he turned the lunch hour meeting into a chat over drinks and arranged to take her to dinner after work.

'We'll have more time to talk,' he suggested.

It was the end of the month and he was short of money, so he took a long time choosing the restaurant and, because Odette Héon was also short of money and was glad to have someone pay for her, she didn't complain. Darcy didn't even apologise but simply explained the situation. It was part of his technique. It was also part of his technique to make sure he took her back to her apartment afterwards when he discovered that the girl with whom she now shared was spending the weekend with her boy friend's family.

'It's not much,' she said as she opened the door. 'It's full of what looks like Louis XIV furniture and isn't. It goes with my car. That looks as if it's Louis XIV, too.'

Darcy studied the flat as she made coffee. 'So this is where it all happened?' he said.

'Where all what happened?' Odette Héon slammed a tray down, complete, Darcy noticed, with a brandy bottle among the cups and saucers. She had clearly taken a fancy to him.

'Dominique Pigny,' he said. 'Whatever she was up to, she probably thought up here. What was she like?'

'Sometimes I thought she was such a bitch it was a wonder she didn't catch rabies. Other times, she was generous, kind and made you laugh. If anybody had a split personality, she did.'

'How was she a bitch?' Darcy asked.

'Well, she pinched the boy I was going out with for one thing. She didn't keep him, though. I think she frightened him to death and he was back panting on the doorstep within a fortnight. I told him where to go. Cognac with your coffee?'

Darcy nodded and found a seat on the settee. It sagged at one end and when she sat alongside him she slipped automatically up against him. They drank their coffee and cognac and Darcy put his arm round her. It was late by this time and she showed no sign of throwing him out.

'I'd better be going,' he said, not moving a muscle.

'You can stay the night, if you like.'

'Where do I sleep?' He jabbed the settee. 'Not on this, surely.'

She laughed. 'It's terrible, isn't it, when men suppress their sexual instincts. They get dreadful headaches.' She picked up her glass and headed for the bedroom. Darcy followed her.

'How do you know I'm not a virgin?' she said.

'They're collector's items these days.'

About two o'clock in the morning, Darcy turned over.

'Dominique la Panique,' he said.

'Oh, not again!' She pulled the sheets up sleepily, then she suddenly came to life and sat up, fully awake.

'Is it true she's dead?'

'As a fish on a slab.'

'What was she up to?'

'That's what I'd like to know. Did you know any of her boy friends?'

'I knew mine.'

'Any others?'

'There was this Paul Pineau she went round with. He keeps a boutique near the Rue Ernest Renan. He calls it "Girl." He would. His mother was English and it shows. He came here with her once. There was also a fisherman in Concarneau. She worked on his boat, she said. I can guess what at, too.'

'I've heard of him,' Darcy said. 'What was his name, do you know?'

'No. But she showed me a photograph of him on his boat. It was called *Petite Annicke*. You could see the name in the photograph. She went over there to see him. About three months ago. She turned up here with what looked like a lot of press cuttings. She had them spread out on the table and she seemed pleased with them.'

'What were they about?'

'They seemed to be about some court case she was interested in. I think she was crazy because the next week she went off to Lyons and came back with some more. She said she'd cut them out of the newspaper files. You aren't supposed to but she'd managed it with nail scissors when the girl who was looking after them went for a coffee. It's the sort of thing she would do. She made me hoot with laughter. She could.' She paused. 'She'd been in trouble, did you know?'

'We heard that. For drugs.'

'A bit more, too. For fraud. Some old man she worked for. She got him to make over some insurances so she could collect them for him, but she kept them, told him they'd lapsed, and vanished with the cash. Something like that. She also did some poor devil for blackmail, too. Did you know that?'

'She has no record. We checked.'

'She was cleverer than you think. The old man with the insurance refused to prosecute, she said, because it made him look a fool and, as for the man she was blackmailing, when he threatened to tell the police she came back with a threat to tell his wife so that was that. She disappeared before he could change his mind. That was before she came to live here, though.' She stopped dead, then went on wonderingly. 'Do policemen always conduct their enquiries in bed?'

'Only if they're with a girl.'

'Are they all like you?'

'Most of them would like to be. My chief, for instance. He's on the slow side. But I once laid on a woman for him – '

'And then laid on her yourself, I expect. Well, you'd better turn over and go to sleep because you're not coming back for seconds. I have to go to work early.'

The following morning Darcy paid a short visit to the police then found Paul Pineau's shop in the shadow of the cathedral.

Pineau was a tall, good-looking man in his forties dressed casually but smartly as though clothes were important to him. His trousers were immaculately cut, his shirt was a primrose yellow, and a red silk scarf was tied negligently at his throat.

'I'm rather busy today,' he said at once. 'My accountant's due.'

'I think you'd better take a break for a moment or two,' Darcy advised. 'I'd like to talk to you about a girl called Dominique Pigny.'

Pineau's face changed and he gestured to the back of the shop. 'I think we'd better go through here,' he said.

He led the way behind a display and pulled a curtain aside so that Darcy found himself in what passed as an office, though, judging by the electric hot plate, the hanging coats, the instant coffee and the carton of milk, it was also where the staff retired for a breather.

Pineau indicated the only chair, lit a cigarette and stood, frowning.

'Dominique Pigny,' Darcy tried. 'When did you last see her?'

Pineau considered. 'A month or two ago? About that. Perhaps a little more. I can't be certain.'

'Where?'

'Here. In Besançon. We met for a meal.'

'How did she get here? Had she transport?'

'Not to my knowledge. I assumed she'd come on the bus or the train. She might even have hitched. It's very possible.'

'Did you know where she was living?'

Pineau didn't know where she was living. She'd arrived in his shop and asked to see him and he'd suggested the meal. He'd been prepared to do the thing in style but she'd chosen an indifferent restaurant which he normally wouldn't have selected.

'I got the impression she didn't want to be noticed,' he said.

Darcy went through the photograph routine and placed the picture of the Lucie necklet on the table. If all had gone as it should, Pineau should have fallen in a dead faint and admitted giving the necklet to Dominique la Panique to buy her affections then murdered her to get it back. Unfortunately, that sort of thing happened so rarely as to be never, and instead he studied the picture carefully, turning it round slowly for a better view.

'It's a Lucie, isn't it?' he said.

Darcy's head jerked round. 'You *know* it's a Lucie?'

Pineau smiled. 'I know a bit about things like that.' He extended his hand. Round his wrist was a gold bracelet, made up of three small chains all roughly the same as the one in the photograph. It went with Pineau. 'That's a Lucie, too,' he said.

'Why are you wearing it?'

'Why do you wear a tie? Why do you wear trousers? It was my mother's originally but these days men wear jewellery too, don't they?'

'I don't.'

Pineau shrugged and fished in his pocket to produce a gold cigarette case. 'Hardly an antique,' he said, 'but it has a history. It was once owned by an aide of Stavisky who in 1934 brought down not one government but two and very nearly started a revolution with his financial machinations.' Fishing in another pocket he produced a gold cigarette lighter. 'No history. No antiquity. Cigarette lighters don't have, do they? But it's valuable.'

Darcy studied him for a moment. 'If I were you,' he said, 'I'd be inclined to keep things like that out of sight. Muggings are increasing every year.'

Pineau gestured at the picture. 'This necklet,' he said. 'Where did it come from?'

'It was Dominique Pigny's. Did you give it to her?'

'Why should I?'

'You knew her well and, since you appreciate the value of good pieces, you could very well have done.'

'I could. But I didn't.'

'Have you seen it before?'

'No.'

'You know she's dead, of course?'

'I saw it in the paper.'

'When you saw her, what did you talk about?'

'Old times. I even thought of asking her to marry me. I knew she'd had an unstable life and I thought I could give her some roots. After all, I'm not poor and I have a house at Andeux. She'd have been very comfortable.'

'Did you ask her?'

'I dropped a hint but she just laughed. It was full of contempt so I didn't bother. She was like that. There wasn't much of her but she knew what she wanted. There were times when I hated her.'

'Why did she come to see you, did you think?'

'Why did she do anything? She was quite unpredictable.'

' "Spooky" she's been described as.'

'That's a good description. Weird. Impulsive. Odd. She probably came because she felt like talking about old times. Or probably just because she knew I'd give her a free meal.'

'She didn't choose a very expensive restaurant, did she?'

'That would be in character. It would be like her to ask for a free meal and decide at the last minute to make it as cheap as possible.'

'Did she mention a man called Gérard Crussol?'

'No.'

'Or a fisherman in Concarneau?'

'No.'

'Did she mention going to Brittany?'

'No.'

'So what do you think she wanted?'

Pineau frowned. 'It was my belief that she just had time to kill and decided she might as well waste my time as anyone else's. She might have been waiting for a bus for all I know. We talked for a while. Here in this office. Then we went out for a meal.'

'And talked of nothing?'

'That's correct.'

Well, it was possible. People did hold conversations that were about nothing and it seemed that anything was likely with Dominique Pigny.

'Did you know she was pregnant?'

Pineau sniffed. 'It would be just like her,' he said. 'She was a very untidy person.'

'It wasn't you?'

'God, no! If I'm nothing else, I'm tidy.'

'Did you sleep with her?'

'Once or twice. At my place. Once when we went for the weekend to Paris. But not lately.' Pineau was silent for a moment. 'She wasn't inexperienced and, given the chance, I think she could have made someone a good wife.'

'What do you mean, given a chance?'

'She was her own worst enemy. She had a lot going for her but she wanted money and she wasn't prepared to get down to it and earn it. She wanted property. She talked of farming.'

'Farming?'

'She seemed to have some project that involved the land. I decided she'd met a farmer who wanted to marry her and she was throwing herself into the idea as disastrously as she threw herself into everything. She'd have made an awful farmer's wife. She'd have forgotten to feed the chickens and failed to lock up the pigs.' Pineau became silent. 'She could have helped me run this business. I'd have been happy to have her.'

'Even if you knew the police were watching her?'

Pineau's face fell. 'Were they?'

'Didn't you know?'

'No.'

Darcy shrugged. 'But then,' he said with a smile, 'she was clever at keeping things to herself, wasn't she?'

When Darcy returned to the Hôtel de Police, Pel was sitting at his desk reading reports. Gautherot had been charged with the theft of Madame Boyer's ducks and they'd got a strong lead about the petrol theft at Loublanc, but Brochard, who had taken over Madame Argoud from Roumy, who'd tried to beat her husband's head flat with a candlestick, could report only that, impervious to pleas, threats and promises, she was still refusing to say why she'd done it.

'There must be a lover boy somewhere.' Aimedieu, who was passing the files across as part of his duties as bodyguard, gave Pel his altar boy look.

As Darcy put his head round the door, Pel gestured to a chair. 'You look as if you'd had all night in with a vampire,' he observed.

Darcy grinned. 'I did. A lady vampire. It's terrible. I don't know how I stand it. There must be something about me, the way they rush at me. I get tired of fending them off. She chased me. Mind, I didn't run very fast.'

Pel didn't approve of Darcy's affairs but there was nothing anyone could do about them. Not even Darcy. He lit a cigarette slowly, stared at it, then hurriedly put it out. 'I keep trying,' he said.

'You could have an operation,' Darcy said.

Pel looked up, a gleam of hope in his eye. 'To stop me smoking?'

'You could have your nose and mouth plugged. You could even have your lungs taken out. But I'm told that's dangerous. People sometimes die after it.'

Aimedieu grinned and Pel glared, but Darcy was unperturbed. 'I've found out a bit more about La Panique,' he said. 'She seems to have been a good liar and not fussy about the niceties of the law. Crussol was certainly right when he said she wouldn't recognise an ethic if she bumped into one. She preyed on people.'

He opened his notebook and began to read. 'Possessing drugs. She got away with that as a first offender. Pushing drugs. She got away with that, too, because she pleaded she was under the influence of drugs at the time and agreed to undergo treatment. She was cured. But then they picked her up for theft. A gold bracelet belonging to her employer. She got away with that one, too. There was also a case of fraud and one of blackmail. I have the details. She probably went in for smuggling, too. She was friendly, it seems, with a fisherman in Concarneau.'

'Name?'

'No name. But I know the name of his boat.'

'You seem to have spent a fruitful time in Besançon.'

Darcy grinned. 'Oh, I did, Patron, I did. What about this fisherman in Concarneau? Do I go there and check him out?'

'Probably.' Pel was curiously non-committal and Darcy frowned.

'Something happened, Patron?'

'Bardolle has an item of news for you.'

'About this?'

'About Philippe Duche. Le Gaston saw what he thought was a poacher in the woods near the Château d'Ivry. He was after something big, he thought, because it wasn't a 6.35 he was carrying.'

Darcy frowned. 'In that case, Patron,' he said, 'I think it's you who ought to go and check this fisherman. You'd then be a long way from Arne. Take Geneviève with you. I'll see that Aimedieu here's within reach all the time.'

'Geneviève isn't going to appreciate that.'

'She won't know.'

'In any case, I'm not sure I ought to take her anywhere with me with this hanging over me.'

'She'll wonder why if you don't, Patron. Besides, I suspect that if she did know she'd *prefer* to be with you.'

Pel considered for a moment, then he nodded. 'Very well,' he said. 'Get Le Bihan to lay it on.'

'Right, Patron. And take your gun. Just in case.'

Pel gave him a sad look. Even Didier Darras was a better shot than he was. 'I'll probably shoot myself in the foot,' he said.

Darcy didn't smile. He looked at Aimedieu. 'How about you?'

Aimedieu patted his gun.

'Just remember what it's for,' Darcy said.

fifteen

Madame Faivre-Perret sounded surprised when Pel put the idea to her.

'Don't you want to go?' he asked nervously.

'Of course I want to go.'

'You're not too busy?'

'Of course, but I'll just ignore it. How are we travelling? In your car?'

'A wheel will probably fall off and you'd end up under a bus. I think we'd better go by train. Anyway, driving all the way across France, we'd arrive worn out. I'll arrange for a hire car to meet us. You won't mind being on your own? What I have to do might take an hour or two.'

'You've only to put me down near the shops and I can pass the time wasting my money. Then when you've finished, we can spend the rest of the day together.'

'I thought we might arrange for a hotel at Benodet. It'll still be quiet there. And they have some excellent restaurants in that area.' Probably special treatment at low prices, too, Pel thought, if they could find one run by one of Le Bihan's cousins.

Going home, he dragged out a suitcase. Madame Routy was still missing and there was a message for him to say she was still on her bed of pain. Clearly she was taking no chances of getting blown up or shot.

It took him all night to pack as he pondered again and again what to take. Twice he unpacked completely, afraid the clothes he had chosen didn't show sufficient decorum or sufficient dash. Waking at dawn, he shaved to the bone then, climbing into his car – carefully avoiding the doors which had a habit of smearing oil over him – he drove to the Hôtel de Police to make sure it hadn't fallen down during the night. Finally, leaving his car, he called a taxi and set off to collect Madame.

She was already at her premises in the Rue de la Liberté, like Pel briefing her staff, and when he turned up he was startled to see them all on the doorstep to wave them off. Pushing her hurriedly inside the taxi, he gave orders for the station, where he saw Aimedieu standing discreetly along the platform. The stationmaster knew Pel and made sure they got a first class compartment to themselves – just in case he ever took up crime and needed Pel on his side – and as they sank back, relieved, with the city sliding away behind them, Pel felt vaguely like some old roué off on a dubious weekend.

When they changed trains in Paris – Aimedieu still not far away – the difference in the weather was already marked. At Le Mans it was raining but at Rennes it had stopped. At Concarneau the rain had disappeared entirely and they began to hope for great things but within an hour a sea fret had come in from the Atlantic and it was possible to hear a foghorn going. Pel was driven to apologise but, to his surprise, Madame seemed quite able to adjust to an unexpected change in the weather. 'After all,' she said, 'we're not going to sit on the beach.'

While Pel was on his way to Brittany, Nosjean, assisted by Claudie Darel, had been occupying himself at Luxeuil. His enquiries were almost the same as those being pursued by Pel about Dominique Pigny but, since his victim had been dead for forty years, they were somewhat more nebulous.

Josée Celine's old colleague and friend from the stage, Nicole Danger, now known as Madame Lazlo Frémion, lived in a small house filled from floor to ceiling with pictures of famous actors and actresses of the period just before, during and after the war, with whom she had appeared.

She was a stout little woman as round as a walnut, white-haired, bright-eyed and cheerful. She had once had a husband but they had parted on friendly terms and had never met since.

'I had no room for a man in my life,' she said cheerfully. 'Not permanently. I had plenty of friends.' She looked sidelong at them. 'Admirers, too,' she added defiantly. 'But nothing to tie me down. I was always too busy.'

Taking out the photographs she'd obtained from Paris, Claudie laid them in front of her.

'Do you recognise these?' she asked. 'They're of the woman found in the caves at Drax.'

Madame Frémion stared at the pictures for a moment then looked up at them. 'Was it Josée they found?' she asked.

'We think so.'

Madame Frémion drew a deep breath like a sigh. 'Well, it's a long time ago. A lifetime. But I ought to recognise them. I was her bridesmaid when she married Xavier Sirdey. He was older than her. A lot older. Was she still wearing his engagement ring?'

Claudie leaned forward. 'There was no ring,' she said.

'Then someone must have taken it from her. She'd never have lost it. It was worth a fortune. It was his mother's, he said, and when she got it she sat with her hand up and her fingers spread out all evening so that everybody could see it. A lot of good it did her. It turned out he was already married. At least my Lazlo didn't do that to me.' She pulled forward a picture of a handsome dark-haired man with a faintly eastern cast of countenance. 'That's him. He was in *Manon* at the time in Nice. The play, not the opera. I played Rosette. He was such a good-looking man and so honest. It was such a pity that after a couple of years I couldn't stand him. Was she wearing her wedding ring? I was with her when they bought it in Paris. We were playing the Bobino at the time. Was she murdered?'

'It seems so.'

'Did Sirdey do it?'

'That's something we're trying to find out,' Nosjean said. 'Can you describe him?'

She could. And did. He was tall, good-looking despite the glasses he wore. He also had a way with him. Enjoying the admiration of women, sharp-tongued, indifferent to other people's opinions, he could, it seemed, have been quite a catch if only he'd been honest.

'No wonder she wasn't wearing her ring,' Madame Frémion said. 'If *he* did it, it would be just like him to remove it. He was like that – careful with money.'

'Would you have a photograph of him?'

She shook her head. Sirdey had a thing about photographs, it seemed. He'd been in the Armée de L'Air during the Great War, and since men who had their photographs taken before a flight never seemed to return, they'd stopped using a camera and Sirdey had said he'd never got rid of the feeling.

'There weren't even any photographs of the wedding,' Madame Frémion said. 'Josée was disappointed but she went along with him.'

She produced a large brown envelope. 'I've picked out some photographs for you. You said you wanted very clear ones and very large ones, and these are the best I could find. They're portraits and publicity pictures. They were taken before she met Sirdey, but only a few months before. Will they help find him?'

'They might,' Nosjean said. Though he had grave doubts. By this time, he felt, Sirdey was doubtless also pushing up the daisies himself.

He studied the pictures. Here and there a well-known face appeared: Maurice Chevalier. Jean Gabin. Jean-Paul Sartre.

Nicole Danger and Josée Celine had been on the fringe of the theatrical greats but never quite part of it.

'It didn't worry me much,' Madame Frémion admitted. 'I was happy. I still am. But Josée always wanted to be someone.'

'She sounds a bit like Dominique la Panique,' Nosjean commented.

'Who's she?' Madame Frémion's ears pricked. 'I never heard of her. It's a queer sort of name for an actress.'

They described the case of the girl dragged from the sea in Brittany and explained the similarity.

'She sounds the same type,' Madame Frémion agreed. 'Josée liked men too much, and she was never very good at picking them. I decided Sirdey was a bad lot straight away. And he was.'

While they were at it, a visit to the area round Drax seemed to be demanded. The house where Sirdey had lived – within five kilometres of the caves – still stood in Dismagnay and, though the occupants had no knowledge of any murder forty years before, they knew of an old man who'd lived down the lane all his life. The old man remembered that just before the woman he'd known as Madame Sirdey had disappeared, he'd seen Sirdey struggling to get a large sacking-wrapped bundle into a van which was parked inside his drive.

He was eighty-seven years old – 'Name of God,' Nosjean said, 'they get older! Any day now, we'll turn up a relic of the Second Empire!' – and hadn't reported the incident at the time, for the simple reason that nobody had asked him.

There was one more call to make – in Talant, in the northern half of the city, where Inspector Bardu, Madame Caous' old admirer, lived. Her description of him – tall and good-looking – still applied. He was seventy-five years old but he was upright and seemed remarkably fit, and they found him sawing logs at the bottom of his garden. He remembered the case of Josée Celine very well.

'It was the biggest thing I ever handled,' he said. 'But we couldn't pin it on Sirdey at all. We went through her belongings, of course, but there was nothing except a few letters that showed she was playing around. There was one from Sirdey accusing her of going with other men, and one she wrote to a man showing she didn't give a damn. It said something about "I'll meet you as usual Friday night after the show at the Hôtel Améon." The Améon was an hôtel de passer. They let rooms by the hour, by the afternoon, by the night, by the day, whatever you wished. She was a cockteaser and probably deserved all she got, and if we'd found the body there'd have been no trouble. But we didn't and now you've found it, *he's* disappeared. It's always the same, isn't it? Things don't change much.'

While Nosjean and Claudie were busy in Luxeuil, Dismagny and Talant, De Troq', his Indian Runners safely disposed of, was making enquiries at a small hotel in Dole where, because of the hostility of the neighbourhood near Drax where he'd lived, Sirdey had stayed for some time following all the brouhaha of the police enquiries. His name, it appeared, had been changed on this occasion from Sirdey to Morot, and the landlady, who had been a girl working for her mother at the time, remembered him well.

'Had you any idea he'd been involved in anything like this?' De Troq' asked.

The landlady sniffed. 'I don't think he was. After all the time I've been in the hotel business, I've learned to judge people, and he was a perfect gentleman. I used to serve him his breakfast in his room. I was only seventeen and pretty, too, and anything could have happened because his room was right at the back where you couldn't hear a thing and there was a big double bed there. But he never attempted anything with me. I was sorry to see him go.'

sixteen

Madame Faivre-Perret was quite happy to look around the shops while Pel drove off in the hired car and sought out the fisherman Darcy had discovered. Le Bihan had made enquiries for him and obtained his name – Charles-Louis LeGrèves.

He was a strong-looking man in his late thirties, swarthy as a gypsy with tight black curls. He wore a fisherman's jersey and thigh boots, and there was a policeman standing alongside his boat.

'To make sure the bastard doesn't disappear to sea,' the policeman explained. 'Inspector Le Bihan's instructions.'

LeGrèves took an aggressive attitude. 'The whole fleet's out except me,' he said. 'Heading for the Cornish coast of England. Your excuse had better be a good one.'

'It is,' Pel said. 'It's a murder enquiry.'

'What stupid con got himself killed?'

'It isn't a him. It's a her. Dominique Pigny.'

LeGrèves frowned, his eyes shifty. 'I read about that in the papers,' he agreed. 'Who did it?'

'Did you?'

LeGrèves glared. 'No, I didn't.'

'But you did know her?'

'No.'

'She went to sea in your boat. How did that miracle happen?'

LeGrèves made an angry gesture. 'Well, yes,' he said. 'I did know her.'

'Why did you say you didn't?'

'I thought you'd think I killed her.'

'I still might.'

'I didn't do it.' LeGrèves was noisily indignant. 'There was nothing to kill her for. Except perhaps her cooking. She couldn't cook to save her life. My engineer and deckhand said that if she stayed, they'd go.'

'And did she stay?'

'Yes. I got a boy to do the cooking and she looked after the engine. She was good with engines. But I didn't kill her. In spite of her cooking. We were always good friends.'

'How good? She was pregnant. Were you that friendly?'

LeGrèves scowled. 'So she was putting it across me,' he said.

'Was it yours?'

'No. I hadn't seen her for some time but she came down here about three months ago and stayed the night at my place. I even asked her to marry me. We got on all right. We never had a cross word except about food.'

LeGrèves' friends seemed to think differently when Pel bought a beer at a nearby café. The fishermen, their clothes marked with salt, were sitting at old-fashioned marble tables and, like most Bretons, were close enough to give little away. But Pet was experienced enough to get them talking and soon discovered that LeGrèves had been seen arguing fiercely with Dominique Pigny.

When he returned to the *Petite Annicke,* LeGrèves was sitting on the foredeck in the sun, making a fender out of unroven coir rope. Le Bihan's policeman sat alongside him, smoking and chatting.

'When are you going to take this stupid con away so I can take my boat to sea?' LeGrèves growled.

'When I'm satisfied I haven't any more questions for you. I've been having a talk with your friends in the bar there. They tell me it wasn't all sweetness and light between you and Dominique.'

LeGrèves directed an angry glance at the bar. 'That's because I pick up more than they do.'

'From fishing?'

'No – yes.'

'Make your mind up. I'll ask you again: Did you kill Dominique?'

'No I didn't. But – '

'But what? Had you reason to?'

'I might have had. After all, she put one across me.'

'What?'

'A little business I did with her.'

'What sort of business? Smuggling? French brandy across to Cornwall? Have you ever tried it?'

LeGrèves hesitated then he grinned. It changed his whole appearance and gave him a mischievous look. 'Once or twice,' he said. 'We get in touch by radio and the Cornishmen meet us with whisky off Finisterre or Land's End. Are you going to charge me?'

'Smuggling's a problem for Customs.'

'Will you pass it on to them?'

'No, I won't. Was Dominique in it with you?'

LeGrèves lit a cigarette quickly and blew out smoke. 'She fixed it. She was quite a girl.' His scowl returned. 'She knew where to get rid of it and she was also clever enough to bolt with the money while I wasn't looking.'

'Is that what she came for?'

LeGrèves looked puzzled. 'Probably. I don't know. She'd certainly got something else on. I don't know what it was. She said she was going to the newspaper office to look something up in their files. Who killed her? Do you know?'

'I thought it might have been you.'

LeGrèves shrugged. 'At the time she disappeared I wouldn't have minded.'

Glancing at his watch, Pel decided he still had time to visit the newspaper office.

As he was shown into the library, he explained he was looking for a young woman who'd been asking three months before to see the files. Because not many outsiders asked for them, the librarian remembered Dominique Pigny well, especially when Pel showed her the copies of the photographs Madame Charnier had supplied.

'She was looking for August, 1970,' she said.

'Would you know what it was she was looking for?'

The librarian wouldn't and Pel sat down with the huge file and started working slowly through the sheets. It seemed a hopeless task but then he remembered that Odette Héon had said Dominique Pigny had cut the files with nail scissors while the librarian wasn't looking and he started turning the sheets more quickly. On August 17th, the page had been defaced and the jagged edges showed where something had been cut out by small-bladed scissors.

The librarian was indignant. 'They're forbidden to deface the files,' she said. 'I wonder how she managed it?'

'What I'm wondering,' Pel said, 'is what it was.'

There were other files and ten minutes later the librarian appeared with another bulky volume. Turning up August 17th, they found that what Dominique Pigny had cut out was nothing more than the report of an inquest on an elderly woman by the name of Simone Cochet, of 17, Rue Dupuy, who had been found dead at the bottom of the stairs by her daughter, Jacqueline.

'Now why,' Pel said aloud, 'would she be interested in that?'

Returning to the city centre with a photocopy of the article, Pel found the police station, identified himself, and asked what was known of Madame Cochet. Records weren't kept there but a middle-aged civilian clerk remembered the case.

'She was old,' he said. 'At first it was thought she'd had an intruder but it was decided in the end she'd heard a noise, got out of bed and fallen down the stairs. It was a big old house and they were steep. She wasn't found until a week afterwards when her daughter called. I can dig out the records but it'll take time.'

'Anything special about the property?' Pel asked. 'Made of gold? Studded with diamonds? Anything like that?'

The clerk grinned. 'Bit tumbledown, as I remember. It's gone now. It was used for a while by the daughter until some charity organisation bought it, then squatters got in there. After that they pulled it down and put up a block of flats in its place.'

Pel nodded, satisfied and, borrowing a telephone, informed Le Bihan what he was doing and arranged for a discreet eye to be kept on LeGrèves. Then, driving back to the shops, he found Madame still quite happy, her arms full of parcels.

It was late afternoon as they drove towards the hotel they'd booked at Benodet. It was a comfortable family hotel, just beginning to open for the holiday season and Pel gallantly gave Madame the room with the better outlook and the bigger bed.

It started raining as they settled in and Pel glared at it. For Darcy, he thought bitterly, it would have been a balmy night with a moon as big as an orange and they'd have been able to stroll hand in hand near the sea. Because it was Evariste Clovis Désiré Pel, it chose to emulate the Flood. Doubtless the Ice Age and the End of the World were just around the corner.

Faintly nervous and unsure of himself, he met Madame for apéritifs in the bar where he went mad and ordered champagne to celebrate their first holiday together. The champagne was just beginning to work and his face had finally become unfrozen when an enormous figure like a badly-set blancmange appeared in the doorway. It was Le Bihan.

'Thought I'd look you up,' he said. 'I can join you for a meal and talk a bit of business. I'm not interrupting anything, am I?'

Pel was all for hitting him over the head with the ice bucket.

Back at the Hôtel de Police the following afternoon, uncertain whether to be depressed by the fact that the arrival of Le Bihan had ruined his evening or elated by the fact that Madame had insisted that she didn't mind so long as she was with him, Pel felt exhausted. Le Bihan had hung on, talking about himself, long enough to spoil the evening and Pel had gone to bed with a feeling of having missed an opportunity.

As he'd undressed, he'd wondered if by chance Madame was expecting him to make a foray down the corridor after the lights went out. Was it possible? Women seemed to expect these sort of things. On the other hand, if she didn't, it could ruin a beautiful friendship. It seemed to call for courage, however, and a touch of élan, and the Pels were not unknown for such things. There must have been a Pel, he felt, leading the attackers at the storming of the Bastille. On the other hand, of course, he had to admit, the family was also noted for its commonsense so it was also very likely that ancestor of his had quietly disappeared down a side street until it was all over.

Nevertheless, the situation had seemed to demand a show of spirit, but the spirit of Evariste Clovis Désiré Pel was obviously not the spirit that had made France great. He had thought about it for a long time and had just reached the conclusion it was worth a try when he had fallen asleep.

He was sitting in his office frowning at a photocopy of the article Dominique Pigny had cut from the newspaper in Concarneau, wondering just what it meant. He had placed it exactly in the middle of his blotter. Now that he'd reached high rank, Cadet Martin felt he should have his blotter changed every morning whether he used it or not and was making great inroads into the Police Authority's stocks of blotting paper. The clean white sheet made the photocopy look almost as if it were in a frame.

Pel frowned. Josée Celine was still only a vague shadow of a person. And what Dominique Pigny had been up to still eluded them. Full of rectitude, Madame Charnier had asked for the body for interment in the family plot, but they still had no idea why Dominique la Panique had telephoned just before her death to say she was coming home. Money? Advice? Charnier himself?

As Nosjean and Claudie appeared round the door, he pushed the photocopy aside and waved them to chairs.

'What about Sirdey?' he asked. 'Has he turned up yet?'

Nosjean shrugged. 'No, Patron. He covered his tracks pretty well. If we could only move forward a step or two, I think we'd sail away. It's the twenty years immediately after getting rid of Josée Celine that have us beaten. We think now that he joined the Milice while the Nazis were occupying the country.'

'Then you have a problem, mon brave,' Pel said. 'You know about the Milice? They worked for the Nazis, and because they were French they knew how French people thought and behaved and were twice as dangerous. And when it was over, most of them vanished as if they'd never existed because everybody was wanting to cut their throats. I think you'll have trouble finding him if he was part of that obnoxious outfit.'

'All the same – ' it was Claudie who spoke this time ' – we think we might have a lead. He went to Dole and we've found a man who might be him called Morot, who married a girl called Henriette Devoise. With her money he bought up a lot of military material when the war ended, much of it American and all of it going cheap. Vehicles. Blankets. Beds. Cooking utensils. Electric light bulbs. Linoleum. Shirts. With the shortages at the time, everybody was crying out for them and he made a small fortune. She died in 1953.'

Pel leaned forward, suddenly interested. 'Of what?'

'Natural causes, Patron.'

'Unless it was "poudre de succession".'

'Inheritance powder?' Claudie looked blank.

'Arsenic. It's very hard to trace and very useful for getting rid of elderly relatives without being found out.'

seventeen

The following day Brochard suddenly cleared up the theft of the petrol at Loublanc, so that, from all the assorted minor crimes they'd been dealing with, they were left only with Madame Argoud, of Roumy, who was still sitting sphinx-like under the interrogations, refusing to say why she had hit her husband over the head with a brass candlestick. Finally, Darcy got a definite sighting of Philippe Duche near Arne. The policeman who saw him was shown photographs and said he'd seen him in Mercourt. He'd been driving a dark blue Peugeot with a smudged number plate and in the back he'd noticed a long, newspaper-wrapped object.

'Gun,' Darcy said. 'The one stolen from Dole.'

Heading back to Mongy, he informed Bardolle what he'd found out and they arranged for help to be available from the substations at Mercourt, Essenet and La Parque while Bardolle posted his men on the high ground overlooking Arne.

Unaware of what was going on in his name, that night Pel stopped his car outside his house in the Rue Martin-de-Noinville to find Didier had turned up again in the hope of another meal. His mother was still busy with her father-in-law and Madame Routy. Pel looked at Aimedieu who, on Darcy's instructions, was still tailing him like a hound-dog.

'You hungry?' he asked.

'I'm just going back to my apartment to cook a banquet, Patron. Out of a tin.'

Pel sighed and jerked his head at Didier. 'Get in,' he said. 'You, too,' he said to Aimedieu. 'Lock your car up. You can pick it up later. We'll eat at the Bar de la Frontière.'

The Bar de la Frontière on the edge of the city was an old haunt of Pel's. It had a dubious clientele of racegoers, lorry drivers and market traders and, in an effort to establish himself as a well-bred, upright, middle-class citizen, he had eschewed it since meeting Madame Faivre-Perret in favour of the Bar du Destin near the Relais St. Armand. The Bar de la Frontière was a dark little place surrounded by horse chestnuts, one of its walls painted with an enormous fading sign 'Byrrh.' It smelled of stale wine and the dining area consisted of a long room filled with scrubbed tables. There was a sandy stretch under the chestnuts where men in blue overalls were playing boules. Children and an old woman with a shopping bag filled with long loaves were watching them and two old men were waving their arms in an argument as if they were about to seize each other by the throat, though entirely without disturbing the tranquillity of the scene. The air was full of a smell of Gauloises that made Pel's nostrils twitch and, Pel was pleased to notice, the blanquette de veau was good – and cheap.

'Have you found out who killed that woman we found?' Didier asked.

'Not yet, mon brave,' Pel said. 'But we will.'

'Do you know who did it?'

'We have an idea. But it was a long time ago and he's moved around a bit since then. How about you? Have you completely recovered from the experience?'

'Oh, yes.' Didier finished his meal and laid down his knife and fork. 'It was nothing, really. Louise is all for me joining the police when I'm old enough. What did he look like?'

'Who?'

'The type who did her in.'

'We'd like to know. He seems to have been very careful never to have his picture taken.'

Didier mopped up his plate with a piece of bread. 'That's a sign of guilt, if ever there was one,' he said.

Pel nodded. It had occurred to him, too.

When he woke the following morning, Aimedieu's car was in the road outside, waiting to follow him to the Hôtel de Police. Pel's throat was sore and he felt strangely lazy, so he invited Aimedieu in and they had a cup of coffee laced with brandy before they left. As they arrived at the Hôtel de Police Darcy appeared. He looked as though he'd been up all night.

'Who was she this time?' Pel asked.

Darcy grinned. 'She was Bardolle,' he said. 'We were doing a bit of a prowl round Arne. Duche's out there somewhere.' He lit a cigarette and drew deeply on it then blew out the smoke in a blue cloud.

'I also saw Le Gaston again,' he said. 'Bardolle says he's a liar and it seems he was even charged with perjury in 1949. But because he's a liar it doesn't mean he's telling whoppers all the time. Bardolle decided that the type he thought was a poacher wasn't after rabbits but after somebody's fat calf. But there was only one man so that rules out calves. He had a description of him. Short, square. Strong-looking. Blond. I reckon, Patron, that Le Gaston was lucky. If he'd tangled with him, he might have got a bullet in the gut for his trouble. I think he stumbled on Philippe Duche.'

Pel said nothing for a moment. He reached out, helped himself to a cigarette from Darcy's packet, lit it with a guilty feeling, and waved away the smoke.

'What now?'

'I'm going across to the Bar Transvaal for breakfast.'

Pel nodded. 'Well, don't take long over it,' he advised. 'I'm going out to Arne again in a minute and you'll perhaps want to be with me. That white Mercedes Le Gaston said he saw still hasn't turned up so he might be lying over that, too. It might be worth checking.'

The lay-by where Le Gaston claimed to have seen the white Mercedes provided an excellent view of the north and west sides of the Château d'Ivry, and as Judge Polverari had suggested, it would have provided a splendid place from which a would-be thief could study the place. On the other hand, a good burglar would have also made a point of finding out about the staffing arrangements and immediately come up with the fact that the Guichets were always around and alert for noises, even during the night. Any house-breaker worth his salt would have turned it down at once as a bad risk.

'And,' Pel observed, staring at the turrets sharp against the sky, 'it occurred to me that if the château was visible from a car, a car would be visible from the château. Perhaps the Guichets saw it.'

Near the entrance to the château the road widened and the trees on the opposite side came down in thick undergrowth from the hill above. Darcy didn't like the look of it and insisted on giving it a quick once-over before allowing Pel to step from the car.

The Guichets were in their room and Pel came to the point quickly. 'The 15th of last month,' he said. 'A white Mercedes car was seen waiting in the lay-by in the road there on that day. Were you in the house at the time?'

'I expect so,' Hubert Guichet said. 'Because of the old man. We have to be here to answer his bell. But I never saw a car.' He glanced at his sister who shook her head. 'We've been here nearly two years and in all that time I don't think I've *ever* seen a car parked down there. There's not much traffic – just between Mongy and Violette – and none of it stops. There's nothing to stop for – only us, and if anybody's coming here they drive straight up to the house.'

'Then why is there a lay-by?'

'It's not a lay-by. It's just that the road was widened early in the century so that carriage horses could take a wide sweep to get into the drive. It's been like that ever since.'

'The car was there on the 15th,' Pel insisted. 'Facing in the direction of Mongy. It was there also on the 14th, the 13th, and probably the 12th. You should have seen it.'

They looked quickly at each other and Bernadine Guichet shook her head.

'This place commands a good view of the road.'

They shrugged and Pel felt his heart sinking. Was Le Gaston a liar about this, too? Was he, as Bardolle had suggested, just trying to draw attention to the fact that his roof needed repairing?

'I'm always being rung for,' Bernadine Guichet was saying. 'And when I go to his room I usually find it's for something quite unimportant. I look out of his window. You can see the whole road from there. I saw nothing.'

She crossed to a small table where a diary lay open. 'I was here all day,' she said. 'We telephoned Doctor Lecomte on the 14th because the old man was complaining of his rheumatism. The doctor said he'd come but he didn't come until the 15th because he knows he's always complaining.' She glanced at the diary. 'I was also in on the 16th, *and* the 17th because the boy who drives the tractor for the farm took the car into Mongy to be serviced. So we were both here for four days in a row. The farmhands could tell you. They must have seen us.'

'What about Monsieur Stocklin? Would he have seen it? I'd like to ask him.'

Mademoiselle Guichet seemed hesitant. 'He won't like being disturbed just now,' she said.

'Why?' Darcy asked bluntly. 'Is this when he does his weight-lifting?'

She studied them for a moment, then shrugged and turned to the door, saying nothing. Her brother followed them in silence.

The noise of the television could be heard going full blast long before they entered Stocklin's room. It sounded like the climax of the Battle of Waterloo. The old man was near the window clutching a blanket round him and holding up his pyjama trousers as if he expected them to fall at any moment round his ankles.

'What are you doing out of bed?' Guichet snapped.

'I was looking through the window.' The old man saw Pel behind Guichet and gave a little cackle of laughter. 'Oh, it's you again, is it?' he said. 'Still not found what you're looking for?'

Pel frowned, faintly depressed by the claustrophobic feeling of the old man's room and the subtle elusive smell of old age.

Mademoiselle Guichet crossed to the television and switched it off. The old man sent up his usual wail of protest.

'I want to watch it!'

'You were looking out of the window and, anyway, it's time for your rest.'

'Leave me alone! Go away! Leave the house! You're fired!'

Mademoiselle Guichet sniffed. 'How will you manage? Who'll cook your meals?'

'I can eat out of tins.'

'You couldn't look after yourself for two days. You're too old. You know you are.'

The old man gave her a savage look and she began to push him to the bed. She obviously knew exactly how to handle him.

As he surrendered, the Guichets began tucking him into bed, using the sheets and blankets almost like bonds to make sure he didn't get out again. His protests were loud and angry and Pel had to wedge his question into a chink in the din.

'On the 15th of the month,' he said, pointing from the window, 'a white Mercedes is supposed to have been parked just down there on the bend. Did you see it?'

'What's he want to know about a car for?' The whining voice was directed at Mademoiselle Guichet.

'I don't know,' she said. 'Perhaps it wasn't there at all. I never saw it.'

'I don't suppose I did either. I don't look for cars. I just watch the road.'

'Why?' Pel's temper, never very stable, was slipping a little. 'What were you looking for?'

The old man heaved in his blankets, muttering to himself. It was impossible to catch what he was saying.

'I said "What were you looking for?" ' Pel repeated.

'It wasn't a what, damn you! It was a who.'

'A who?' The room had suddenly become silent and Pel straightened up and looked at Darcy. 'A person?'

'Yes.'

'Who?'

The old man's face appeared above the bedclothes. His cheeks were flushed with anger and exertion and his faded eyes were curiously bright.

'I was looking for Sidonie,' he snarled.

eighteen

The sudden silence was thick enough to cut with a knife. Pel glanced again at Darcy then he moved nearer to the bed. The Guichets were watching carefully.

'Sidonie *who*?' Pel asked.

The old man glared at him. 'Sidonie Charnier,' he said.

His spectacles had obviously been discovered because this time they were on the table by the bed and Pel gestured at Darcy. 'The pictures, Daniel,' he said quickly.

Darcy produced the copies of the pictures Madame Charnier had provided. As Pel showed them, the old man's face lit up at once.

'That's her!'

'Her name's Pigny, Monsieur,' Pel pointed out. 'Dominique Pigny. Did you know her?'

'Of course I knew her. She worked here. I liked Sidonie. She was a good girl. She liked me, too. I know she did.'

Pel turned to the Guichets. The woman's eyes were worried.

'Nobody by the name of Dominique Pigny ever worked here,' she said quickly. 'She said her name was Sidonie Charnier.'

It made sense if Dominique Pigny were trying to hide but it still needed an explanation. 'I showed you photographs,' Pel said. 'You must have recognised her.'

She shrugged. 'They were bad photographs. Bad photographs take all the life out of a face.'

'These were very *good* photographs,' Pel snapped. 'Her sister – by the name of Sidonie Charnier, by the way – vouched for them.'

He drew the Guichets to the other side of the bedroom out of earshot of the old man. 'Why did you hide the fact that she worked here? She did, didn't she?'

Bernadine Guichet sighed. 'Yes,' she admitted. 'She worked here.'

'Then why not say so?'

'She left just over a month ago. On the 15th of last month. Just walked out on us. I always thought she might. She was quite unreliable.'

'Where did she go?'

'She set off to catch a bus to Mongy.'

'She never got there. Why did you insist she didn't work here?'

Mademoiselle Guichet looked at her brother who shifted uneasily on his feet. 'She asked us not to let anyone know. She said she wanted to mind her own business. We didn't argue. It wasn't easy to get people to work here. She was different. She was odd – secretive. She never went into the village and she never told us where she came from or what she did in her spare time.'

'What do you *think* she did?'

Mademoiselle Guichet shrugged. 'Men, I suppose. That's usually the case at that age. I thought she might have been involved in something else, too – something dishonest – especially when she asked us not to let anybody know where she was. I didn't like the idea of employing someone who might be involved in criminal activities, and I got the impression that there was a man and that she was hiding from him. We were just anxious to keep her here, despite her being so strange.'

'She's dead,' Pel snapped. 'She's been murdered. I made that clear.'

Mademoiselle Guichet gestured feebly. 'I thought some criminal might come. Something like that. I thought it was best to go on saying nothing.'

'She wasn't sacked?'

'No. But she would have been.'

'Why?'

'Her job was to help in the kitchen and carry the food up here. To save my legs. Then I noticed she was staying longer up here than she need, and I discovered she was making up to him.'

'The old man? How?'

'How *do* women make up to old men?'

'Inform me.'

'She was telling him she was younger than she was, and he was too old and short-sighted to tell her age. He started to give her money.'

'What for?'

She shrugged, leaving the answer unspoken.

'After *she* came,' Hubert Guichet said, 'he started sending me down to the bank at Mongy for cash. She showed me a dress he'd paid for. He probably gave her other things we never heard about.'

Darcy held out the photograph of the Lucie necklet. 'Such as this? She was wearing it when she was found.'

Guichet frowned. 'I don't know. I never saw it before.'

'These gifts,' Pel said. 'What were they in return for?'

Bernadine Guichet's voice was low as she answered. 'Surely you can guess.'

'He's an old man.'

'Even old men feel young at times. I've looked after a lot. You'd be surprised. Sometimes they seem to have six pairs of hands. She read to him. Once I found her lying beside him on his bed.'

'Doing what?'

'Holding him. She said he was cold. But she was close to him.' Mademoiselle Guichet looked shocked. 'I decided it was becoming dangerous, and thought she was after his money. It's happened before with old men.'

The old man's voice broke in over the whispered questions and answers from the other side of the room. 'When's Sidonie coming back?' he said.

'Her name wasn't Sidonie,' Guichet said over his shoulder. 'The Chief Inspector here says it was Dominique.'

'She told me it was Sidonie. When is she coming back? She said she would.'

Guichet began to pile pillows round the old man. 'All these pillows,' he said, clucking like an old hen. 'One day you'll turn over and drown in them.'

The old man gave him a bitter look. 'You said I should have them.'

'You were complaining of rheumatism. It's not necessary now. But, if you insist – '

'I don't insist.'

Guichet frowned. 'I never know where I am with you.'

'What about Sidonie?'

'She's left.'

The old man's voice rose in a wail. 'Sidonie understood me! She knew what I liked and what I wanted!' A pair of faded eyes fell on Pel. 'Why are the police here again? I don't think much of the police. They couldn't find a lost dog. I want Sidonie. She used to sit with me for hours.'

'She also used to lie on the bed with you,' Mademoiselle Guichet snapped.

The old man's whine grew sharper and brisker. 'What's wrong with that?' he asked.

'Perhaps even *in* the bed.'

The old man cackled. 'You'd love to know, wouldn't you?'

'You're a dirty old man.'

'Yes, I know. I'd have had *you* in here, too, before now, except that you're not my type.'

Mademoiselle Guichet looked furious and the old man cackled again. 'And you'd have come, too, if you'd thought I'd marry you. You'd have been glad to get your hands on my money.'

Mademoiselle Guichet gave an angry snort. 'Marriage isn't possible at your age!'

'You don't know my family.'

They didn't have to go to Doctor Lecomte to confirm what Bernadine Guichet had said. The tractor driver at the farm agreed that he'd taken the station wagon for two days' work on it at Mongy and that he'd seen the Guichets about the place all the time during those days and the days before.

Pel was silent as they headed for the car. His head was beginning to ache and he decided it was the concentrated thinking he was doing. He was even beginning to grow a little tired of Dominique Pigny. She never quite seemed to come to life and he still wasn't sure what she'd been like. But, if nothing else, they'd learned that she'd been at the Château d'Ivry and that when she'd left on the 15th, the day Le Gaston had seen her, she'd not intended to stay away long.

'It's obvious old Stocklin likes women,' he said.

'All men like women,' Darcy said. 'The old ones over a cup of coffee. The younger ones in bed. It's a natural phenomenon.'

Pel frowned. 'Was she blackmailing him, do you think? He was giving her money and she'd tried blackmail before.'

'It seemed to me,' Darcy said, 'that if he gave her the money, he gave it freely.'

'Then was she blackmailing someone else?'

'If she was, then that's who must have killed her. It couldn't have been the Guichets because when she was killed they were at the Château and they couldn't possibly have been away without being missed for two days – which is what it must have taken to cart her to Beg Meil and dump her in the sea.'

Pel frowned. *And*, he reminded himself, despite knowing its number and its owner, the white Mercedes they were seeking, the white Mercedes which had carried Dominique Pigny's body to Brittany, still hadn't turned up.

However, it was about to.

nineteen

At lunchtime at the Relais St. Armand, between the hors d'oeuvres and the coq au vin, with Aimedieu gloomily sucking his teeth in his car outside and thinking of tinned mince, Pel chose to be funny to Madame Faivre-Perret.

'I've found the perfect place for Madame Routy,' he said cheerfully as he sat back. 'Old boy out at Arne. Watches television all day, isn't fussy what he eats, and doesn't care whether the place's clean or dirty. She could feed him on casseroles and watch with him.'

Madame smiled. 'I've got plans for Madame Routy,' she said.

'Don't tell me you've found somewhere for her to go.'

Madame was smiling. 'Yes,' she said. 'I've found somewhere.'

'*Where*? North Pole? South Africa? Siberia?'

Madame smiled. 'She can look after *us*.'

Pel dropped his fork. 'Look after us!' The thought of Madame Routy pursuing him into married life was enough to make an Ethiopian go pale. 'Not Madame Routy,' he said in shocked tones.

'Why not?' Madame asked mildly. 'Housekeepers are hard to get these days and we'll need someone to run the place.'

'She can't cook! And she'll watch television all day!'

'She'd better not.'

'You don't know her.'

'All to the good.' Madame seemed quite confident. 'I shall be able to handle her better.'

Pel headed back to his office, feeling his future had been blighted. The thought of Madame Routy running his marital establishment was enough to destroy the confidence of the strongest man. Within weeks, she'd be back to her old habits and more than likely have Madame Faivre-Perret cowering, too. On the other hand, he had to admit, Madame Faivre-Perret seemed to have hidden resources. And if she could run an establishment like Nanette's she must have courage. To charge the prices Nanette's charged she *had* to have courage.

He arrived back at the Hôtel de Police feeling much better. Perhaps, he thought, Madame Faivre-Perret would be able to handle Madame Routy after all. You never knew, it might be Madame Routy who would be doing the cowering. After so many years of strife with her, the idea pleased him, and he actually smiled to himself. But as he reached his room, his self-satisfaction died at once. His department was in uproar. The white Mercedes they'd been seeking for so long had finally turned up – by accident.

'In a lock-up garage at Dampierre,' Darcy said. 'The police there have drug problems and when they put on a snap search for hidden caches in warehouses, sheds and garages, there it was. The number's correct. It's the dentist's all right and it has a damaged headlight and wing.'

Pel was adjusting quickly from his mood of euphoria to one of immediate alertness.

'Who owns the garage?' he snapped.

'Type called Grassart. He's straight and has no record. He's a pensioner and has a row of garages he lets off to add to his income. Somebody rented one and paid him for four months, saying he'd come back with his car that night.'

'Description?'

'Same as we got from Le Gaston. White suit, blue shirt, white tie.'

'Anything inside the car?'

'An empty can of de-icer, a notepad, a dirty duster, a pair of sunglasses, a red crayon pencil, and a set of Michelin maps in a plastic envelope. All the owner's. There was also a map that isn't his – of the Grandes Routes de France, with circles on it round Mongy, Arne and Benodet, and a route marked in the red crayon across country from Arne via Avallon, Orléans, Le Mans and Rennes, avoiding all main roads.'

'Fingerprints?'

Darcy grinned and Pel guessed he was saving the best bit for last. 'In addition to the owner's and his wife's and daughter's, they found dabs which have been identified as belonging to one Marie-Josephe Danot, also known as l'Aixois because he was born in Aix-en-Provence, and as Jo-Jo la Canne because he broke a leg as a young man – or had it broken for him by some of his friends in Marseilles – so that he has to use a walking stick. Heard of him?'

Pel sniffed. 'Demi-sel,' he said. 'Small-time crook. Gangster and racketeer in and around Marseilles. Involved in protection rackets and a few other things.'

Darcy nodded. 'Worked at one time with the Berlioni gang. Suspected of the murder of one of the opposition, Antonio Latoni, known as Tony the Tout, and also of the killing in Toulon of one Marie Topin, a prostitute. They were both gang murders and the Marseilles police were certain Jo-Jo did them both but could never pin them on him.'

Pel frowned. 'Did *he* know Dominique Pigny?'

'We'll know that better when we find him. His mother lives in Rochefort. I've contacted police headquarters and asked them to keep an eye on the house.'

Pel sat down slowly in his chair, and pushed his spectacles up on his forehead. They nestled among the thin hair at the front of his skull like two pigeon's eggs in a very sparse nest.

'Jo-Jo la Canne,' he said slowly. 'He killed her and took her in the car and dumped her in the sea at Benodet so that the body turned up with the tide in Beg Meil. But why?'

'She was pregnant, Patron.'

'By Jo-Jo la Canne?' Pel shook his head. 'She doesn't seem the sort who goes with him. And he doesn't seem the sort who goes with her.'

Late in the afternoon, they learned two new facts. The damage to the Mercedes found at Dampierre was consistent with causing the injuries from which Dominique Pigny had died and the boot showed traces of blood. Doctor's records showed it to be the same group as Dominique Pigny's – which supported the theory that she'd been killed near Arne and taken the same night to Benodet to be dumped in the sea. Doubtless Jo-Jo la Canne had driven throughout the night, clearly wishing to put as much distance as possible between himself and the scene of the crime, but, because he'd arrived after daylight and was noticed by the mother of a small boy giving a party, he'd been forced to wait all day in and around Benodet until darkness to get rid of the body in the sea. The second fact, equally important but more unhelpful, was that Jo-Jo la Canne had not been seen near his mother's house in Rochefort.

Pel was thoughtful. He was still working on the theory that Dominique Pigny, despite her oddness and her undoubted dishonesty, didn't go with Jo-Jo la Canne. Jo-Jo was a vicious type. So far, Dominique just seemed a little unbalanced, a type who would do anything for a laugh or for money, or to irritate the more formal people of the world.

'We seem to have established,' he said, 'that she *was* walking down the road from Arne past the spot where Le

Gaston was working and that Jo-Jo *was* waiting for her. He couldn't have been waiting to pick her up because he'd been there three days in succession. So where was she going? And why was she going there? And *why* did Jo-Jo la Canne run her down and kill her? What was *his* interest in the affair?'

Pel was due to see Madame again that evening to discuss the plans for their future. With the certainty that Duche was still at large, Darcy was none too keen, but as it happened the matter was resolved very simply. During the afternoon Pel began to feel off-colour so that even the cigarettes he smoked tasted foul, and in the end he called on Doc Minet on the excuse of asking if anything more had turned up on Josée Celine and persuaded him to have a look at him.

'It's bog spavin,' Doc Minet said, his plump face amused. 'It's a disease in horses.' Minet's eyes danced. 'You've obviously got a cold coming on. If I were you I'd go home and get into bed.'

Convinced he was dying, Pel telephoned Madame to say what had happened. The concern in her voice made him feel it was almost *worth* dying.

'Go to bed,' she said. 'With a hot water bottle.'

He found Madame Routy had grown tired of being ill and, convinced that it was now safe to emerge, had returned and was watching the television. The noise brought on a splitting headache of the sort reserved for sufferers from sinusitis.

'Turn that thing down,' Pel said.

'I'm just watching the end of this,' Madame Routy said.

She was always just watching the end of something. If she'd lived during the Revolution, she'd have been sitting by the guillotine, knitting herself silly as she watched the last of the day's batch of aristocrats being topped.

'I think I have pneumonia,' Pel snarled. 'I'm going to bed, and if it disturbs me I shall come downstairs and kick the front in.'

About the time that Pel was sinking into unconsciousness, a young business executive was making love to a woman in large brand-new six-cylinder Peugeot 604 which he'd driven just inside a small ride in the Forêt de Diviot near Sombernon. He had a wife of his own age who was kind, good, devout and hardworking, but she was dull and the young man liked fun and the idea of making love to another man's wife – especially a woman whose husband held a position of great wealth and importance – was exciting to him. She had telephoned him that afternoon that her husband had flown to Toulon on business and wasn't due back until the following morning.

The young man had dressed in his best suit – the one he kept for weddings, dinner parties, meeting important businessmen and seducing women. He was a powerfully-built young man who prided himself on his masculine virility, and as they combed out and buttoned up, he was feeling very pleased with himself. It had been a pleasant evening out, paid for by the woman, who was eager for excitement because she felt she was growing old and had little time to waste, and he was quite prepared now to go home to his loving, hardworking, dull wife, who thought he was on his way back from Paris after a business trip and wasn't expecting him until midnight.

It was with a feeling of satisfaction that, chattering cheerfully, he climbed behind the driving wheel of the big Peugeot, started the engine and put it into reverse. Pleased with himself, he swung the wheel with a certain amount of panache to show what a devil he was and put his foot on the accelerator, so that the big car swung round in a swift half-circle to face the road. Unfortunately, in his self-satisfaction, the young man was showing off and was a little too enthusiastic. Just as he was about to apply the brakes preparatory to engaging forward gear, he felt a bump and a crunch and the car came to a stop, one of the rear wheels in a half-obscured ditch that bordered the road.

'Holy Mother of God,' he said.

Climbing out of the driving seat, he took a torch from the pocket and went to the rear of the car. The ditch was deep and full of leaves and small branches that were a relic of winter gales. The car was resting with its chassis on the bank and, angry at his carelessness, he grasped the bumper and lifted. But the Peugeot was too heavy even for his strong shoulders. He strained until he began to think he might rupture himself then, still angry with himself but certain he could overcome the problem, he climbed back into the driving seat and, putting it into forward gear, pressed the accelerator. There was a screaming sound as the wheels revolved.

The woman gestured nervously. 'Try it more slowly,' she said.

He tried it more slowly. It made no difference.

'You drive it,' he said. 'I'll push.'

As she slipped into his place, he climbed into the ditch and put his shoulder against the car. When nothing happened, she increased the pressure on the accelerator and as the wheels spun, twigs, dead leaves, grass and wet soil were flung over the young man's splendid suit.

'Name of God!' he yelled. 'Lay off that accelerator! Look at me!'

By this time both of them were growing anxious and their anxiety was making them angry. As the young man began to curse in words that startled the woman, in her own anger she responded bitterly.

'There's no need to talk like a peasant,' she said.

The young man sourly brushed the dirt off his suit. 'There's a village down the road,' he said. 'I'll get someone to come up with a tractor and a rope.'

'They'll be in bed. Suppose they won't come?'

The young man looked worried. 'We'll have to walk home.'

'Do you realise how far it is? And what do we do about the car?'

The young man was now beginning to experience a distinct sinking feeling in the pit of the stomach. If they didn't reach home some time during the night – and if they had to walk they undoubtedly wouldn't – questions would be asked. And that would be awkward because the car was his boss' and the woman was his boss' wife.

'I'll try,' he said, aware for the first time that one of his clever little schemes had gone wrong.

The woman had the torch now and was shining it along the ditch, in the forlorn hope of finding stones or a log to thrust under the rear wheel to give it sufficient purchase to drive out of the ditch.

'Wait!' Her voice was suddenly urgent and shrill with a note of panic and she began to back away from the car, the torch still held in front of her.

'Oh, my God!' she said and the way she said it brought the young man leaping to her side.

'What's the matter?'

She gave him a stricken look, partly fear, partly anxiety.' 'There's a man there,' she breathed. 'And he's dead!'

twenty

Pel slept fitfully, his mind a whirl of details. The Pigny and Celine cases were beginning to get on top of him, he realised, and, unable to put them from his mind, he reached for the whisky bottle because Doc Minet had once told him that people who took sleeping pills would do better to try that. In the early hours he woke, saturated with sweat, startled at the amount he'd drunk.

Coming to consciousness the following morning, he peered warily over the sheets, expecting to see the day rushing at him. But the room was quiet and he even began to feel a little better. Then the Pigny and Celine cases came back at him and he heaved in bed, knowing he ought to go to work but feeling like a schoolboy with a sniffle who hadn't done his homework properly and was pretending to be more sick than he really was.

In the end, he rose, and moving slowly, went downstairs. He was later than usual and Madame Routy had already disappeared to the shops. She had placed his cup and saucer on the table and left the coffee pot on the cooker. The coffee tasted like being hit in the face with a wet football so he started to make himself a fresh cup with instant powder, feeling that no matter how bad it was, it would inevitably be better than Madame Routy's. He was standing in the kitchen, holding a piece of soggy croissant, when the telephone went. It was Madame Faivre-Perret.

'What are you doing up?' she demanded at once. 'You should be in bed.'

He meekly promised to go back to bed at once and not move for forty-eight hours.

'And just see that Madame Routy makes you some good appetising food. Something light but tasty.'

He promised, knowing full well that whatever Madame Routy attempted, it would inevitably turn out as a casserole as heavy as lead.

'You promise?'

'I promise,' he said. 'I'll go as soon as I've finished my coffee.'

He didn't know what was coming.

He was still in the kitchen when the telephone went again. He crossed to it, moving like an old man, and stood holding the telephone in one hand and his soggy croissant in the other.

'Patron – ' it was Darcy's voice ' – we think we've turned up Jo-Jo la Canne!'

'What?' Pel almost choked as a fragment of croissant went down the wrong way.

'Forêt de Diviot. In a ditch covered with leaves and old branches. Found by a type called Yves Cerussier, who happened to be out there with his boss' car *and* a woman called Husson who happens to be his boss' wife. They're looking pretty sick, because it looks as though *he's* going to lose his job and *she's* going to lose her husband. Jo-Jo was shot.'

'I'll be down. Hold everything.'

'Hang on, Patron,' Darcy said. 'Are you fit? I only rang up to let you know what was going on. I can handle things.'

Pel stared at the telephone as if he expected a toad to jump out of it.

'I said hold everything,' he snarled. 'Pick me up in ten minutes.'

He scrambled upstairs, falling over his dressing gown cord, and washed and dressed at full speed. His head felt as if the side was dropping off but the knowledge that things were happening bore him up.

Darcy appeared within minutes and, picking up enough spare cigarettes as they left the city to last Pel through a siege, they headed for Sombernon. The police had already placed a screen just to the rear of the Peugeot which still stood with one of its rear wheels overhanging the ditch. Cerussier and Madame Husson were sitting in the car belonging to the police brigadier from Sombernon. They were no longer on speaking terms. Around the Peugeot were police, fingerprint experts and men from the forensic laboratory. There was even a reporter and a photographer who had materialised from nowhere and, quick to sense a scandal, had whipped off a few useful pictures of Cerussier and Madame Husson.

As Pel approached them, they were both sunk into gloom, Cerussier wondering what story he could tell his wife, what story he could tell his employer, and finally what it would be like without a job. Madame Husson was wondering how much blame she could throw on Cerussier and whether her husband would believe it if she suggested she'd been abducted? She thought it most unlikely.

Pel studied them for a moment then walked to where Doc Minet was gingerly moving leaves and twigs and small branches. In one spot they had been heaped up into a pile and Minet was carefully picking them up, almost one by one. In the ditch, still half covered, was the huddled body of a man. There was blood across his face and one of his hands as though he had clutched at his wound in the moment he died. He was dressed in a cream-coloured suit with a dark blue shirt and a white tie. Beneath him lay a walking stick with an ivory handle.

'That's Jo-Jo all right,' Darcy said.

'What happened?' Pel asked.

'Two bullets,' Doc Minet decided. 'Both entrance wounds in the left side of the head. I can't tell you the calibre yet but it looks like a 6.35mm. He was shot here. There are wheel marks right alongside the ditch there.'

'When?'

'About forty-eight hours ago, I'd say.'

Policemen from the Sombernon substation and neighbouring villages were combing the undergrowth for anything that might be a help. The brigadier in charge had laid a large handkerchief on a flat stone and had the contents of the dead man's pockets spread out on it.

'Wallet containing fifty francs,' he said. 'A few coins. Handkerchief. Cheque book issued by the Crédit Lyonnais bank in Rochefort. Penknife. Car keys. What looks like a house key. Cigarettes. Lighter. And that's about all.'

'Get in touch with Crédit Lyonnais,' Pel said. 'Tell them it's a murder enquiry. We need his address.'

By lunchtime, with Yves Cerussier and Madame Husson in their respective homes at last, both engaged in long explanations of what they'd been up to, Pel was outside Jo-Jo la Canne's address in Rochefort. His mother, it seemed, had been in hospital for over a year and he had taken rooms to be near her.

The apartment was a bachelor affair with no feminine touches, many dirty dishes in the sink and a lot of dust. Jo-Jo la Canne might have been a bit of a dandy when he was out and about but at home he lived a slovenly existence.

His landlady who lived on the ground floor didn't hold a very high opinion of him. 'He owes me rent,' she said. 'When I asked him for it two nights ago he said he was just on his way to collect some money that was owing to him. He used my telephone to talk to someone and went out saying he'd pay me next morning. He never came back.'

There was no indication of whom it was Jo-Jo had met, but when Lagé, Misset and Debray tore the apartment apart, it revealed small quantities of hallucinatory drugs and a letter which indicated that, in addition to his other activities, Jo-Jo had been the salesman for the manufacturer, who appeared to be a research student using one of the laboratories at the university. There were names and addresses, even a run-down on methods.

By late afternoon, in addition to the landlady's, Prélat, of Fingerprints, had found the dabs of Jo-Jo, one or two unknowns and three students at the university who by this time were answering questions at the police station.

As might have been expected, Jo-Jo hadn't been in the habit of eating at home and his dustbin, which hadn't been emptied for weeks, contained nothing more than a few scraps of paper, among them the torn fragments of Dominique Pigny's identification papers and driving licence, and two crumpled press cuttings. Carefully, Pel spread the cuttings out on the table. One was the same as the Xerox copy he'd had made in Concarneau concerning the death of Madame Cochet. The other concerned the funeral of a wealthy cancer patient in Lyons by the name of Raoul Zeller, of 41, Avenue Maréchal Lebrun. Like the identification papers and the driving licence, they had clearly come from Dominique Pigny's handbag, which Jo-Jo la Canne, never one to miss an opportunity, had doubtless sold or given to a girl friend.

'Now, why,' Pel asked, 'was she interested in an old woman called Simone Cochet in Concarneau and a man in Lyons suffering from terminal cancer called Zeller?' He sniffed and pushed his spectacles up on to his forehead. 'And did Jo-Jo give her that necklet?'

'Could he afford it, Patron?' Darcy asked. 'And would he have that much taste? If Jo-Jo had wanted to buy a girl something of that value, I'd have said it would be big and vulgar.'

Returning to the Hôtel de Police, they found that yet another of the minor thorns in their flesh had been cleared up. Brochard had been having another go at Madame Argoud, from Roumy, who had tried to hammer her husband's head flat with a brass candlestick. After days as silent as a Trappist monk she had suddenly blurted out the reason.

'It was because he snored,' Brochard said. He was young and inexperienced and he looked faintly bemused. 'She said she'd listened to him for fifteen years and suddenly she decided she was sick of it.'

It was another victory – only a small one, true, because the thing they were really after now was the identity of the person with whom Jo-Jo had spent his last hours alive – but a victory nevertheless, and, feeling like death again now that the excitement had died, Pel was just considering going home when Lagé appeared.

'We've found the gun that shot Jo-Jo, Patron,' he announced. 'The army turned up with a mine-detector and found it down a rabbit hole. It's an MAS 6.35mm with the initials "OF" scratched on the barrel.'

'Who in God's name is "OF"?' Pel growled. 'We've got no one we're interested in with those initials.'

That night, Pel knocked himself out with a sleeping pill, and woke the next morning feeling as if he were trying to drag himself up out of a bed of treacle. He felt dreadful and he knew he hadn't kept his promise to Madame about taking care, but there was a feeling in his bones that they were on the brink of something, and, being Pel, he couldn't bear the thought of somebody stumbling on it before he did.

Aimedieu picked him up and drove him to the office, his mind still busy. If Jo-Jo la Canne had killed Dominique Pigny accidentally, as was still very possible, then his panic was understandable. But had he? You didn't wait for three days in a lay-by to have an accident. And if it weren't an accident, then *why* had he killed her? And, having done so, why had Jo-Jo himself been killed? And by whom?

Sitting at his desk, he chewed over the details. It wasn't easy, because his cold was beginning to make him feel as if everything about him was clouded.

Leguyader and Doc Minet appeared just before lunch, looking like twin angels of doom.

'Marie-Josephe Danot,' Leguyader said. 'Known as Jo-Jo la Canne. His clothes tell us very little but there's one thing we know with certainty: He didn't get out of the car that took him to where he was found until he was pushed out. And then he went head-first, which suggests he was already dead. There are no traces of leaves or soil from the Forest of Diviot on his shoes so we think he was picked up somewhere – perhaps arranged by that telephone call of his – and driven to the forest on the grounds that it was lonely and they wouldn't be recognised. Also, of course, because when dead he wouldn't be found for some time. It's a pity for whoever murdered him that Cerussier happened to choose that spot for his romp with Madame Husson.'

Minet produced a plastic bag containing a small fragment of misshapen metal. '6.35 bullet,' he said. 'From Jo-Jo's head. There were a lot of 6.35s about after 1945 and a lot disappeared into private cupboards. This one was held up against Jo-Jo's head, because there are scorch and powder marks. The entrance wound's in the left temple and there's another through the hole of the left ear. That one came out through the right temple, taking off part of the side of the skull and face. Since the entrance wounds are on the left side, Jo-Jo was probably a passenger in the front seat and was shot twice in rapid succession by the driver. It would be very easy. Unlike the British, who are crazy and drive on the wrong side of the road, the steering wheels in our cars are on the left side of the car, so, if the driver was right-handed, which most people are, all he had to do was bring the weapon from his pocket and it would be over before Jo-Jo knew what was happening. There are no signs of a struggle. No broken nails. No bruises. After he'd shot him, I think the driver simply reached across the body, opened the door and pushed him out. If the car was parked with its wheels on the edge of the ditch – and judging by the tyre marks it was – then he'd fall into the ditch and it would be a simple matter to cover him with dead leaves and drive away.'

Leguyader shuffled a group of photographs he'd brought along. 'That's a picture of the bullet taken from his head. And *that's* a photograph of a bullet fired from the gun found in the rabbit hole. They match.' He indicated the plastic bag. 'Find the owner of that gun,' he said, 'and you have the man who killed Jo-Jo la Canne.'

As Doc Minet and Leguyader vanished, Pel lit a cigarette. His cold – only he could get a cold in the middle of summer, he decided bitterly – was growing worse and he was hoping for the rest of the day to be quiet so he could snatch himself back from the jaws of death. But the door had hardly closed when Darcy appeared. He was red-faced with hurrying.

'Arne,' he said. 'I was checking on Philippe Duche with the foreman for that farm the château runs, and he let it drop that a man who answers to Crussol's description was there not long before Dominique La Panique disappeared.'

Pel peered at him, alert despite watering eyes. 'With the girl?'

'On his own. He said he'd come to buy potatoes. He'll need seeing, Patron. I'll get my car.'

twenty-one

Bardolle was waiting just down the street from Crussol's house.

'He's in,' he said.

The door was opened by Crussol who, for a change, looked clean. He was dressed in a dark suit and was struggling to knot a black tie round his neck.

'Sorry,' he said at once. 'Can't stop now.'

'You can stop for ten minutes,' Darcy snapped.

'There's a funeral come up. It was my day off but they've called me in. We've got to box a stiff.'

He was about to close the door when Bardolle took a hand. Placing an enormous fist on Crussol's chest, he pushed him back into the house and closed the door behind them. Although Crussol was taller, there appeared to be more of Bardolle and Crussol sighed and gave way. Leading them to the garage, he began pouring beer at once. Jesus was still raising Lazarus from the dead but Lazarus' feet seemed to have changed shape and even appeared to be deformed.

Pel came to the point at once. 'Arne,' he said.

Crussol seemed to shrink. 'What about it?'

'You were there around the 10th of last month. We have a witness.'

'It wouldn't be me.'

Pel produced the map they'd found in the white Mercedes and indicated the circles round Mongy, Arne and Benodet.

Crussol looked scared. 'Whose is it?'

'Why?'

'Just asked.'

'As a matter of fact, it came from a car driven by one Jo-Jo la Canne, a petty gangster, thief, con man and suspected murderer – now dead. Dominique Pigny was living at Arne just before she died.'

Crussol shook his head violently. 'I didn't know.'

Pel's finger rested again on the map. 'Benodet's next door to Beg Meil where she was found dead. Mongy's where you met her in the café. Rather a coincidence, I think. Can you explain it?'

'No, I can't.'

'What about this man who was seen at the château? The one who looked like you?'

'It wouldn't be me. I'd be at work.'

'We'll check with your boss.'

Crussol seemed to panic. 'Look,' he said, 'I did take the day off about then. I'd been working too hard. Probably got psillicosis from hacking away too much at stone. You *can* get it, you know. I needed a day in the country. I might have gone there. Just wandering about. You know how you do. But I didn't know Dominique was living there. It would be just by chance.'

'You'll have to do better than that, my friend,' Darcy said.

'Look – ' Crussol lifted his hands as if warding them off – I'll tell you what happened. It was Dominique's idea.'

'What was?'

'The old boy at the château. He was worth a fortune. When she got the job there, she suddenly realised what she was on to. She asked me to meet her so I arranged to see her in the woods across the road. But this type on a tractor saw me and I had to spin him a yarn about looking for cheap potatoes.'

'Why did she want to see you?'

'To tell me what she was doing.'

'What was she doing?'

Crussol made a sheepish gesture. 'Well,' he said, 'I must admit *I* thought she was on to a good thing, too. The old boy had taken a fancy to her. He said she reminded him of his first wife and started getting sentimental whenever she appeared with his food. He got her to read to him. Sometimes they talked. Then he complained about feeling cold, so she lay on the bed with him and held him to warm him up.'

'An old man?'

Crussol managed a nervous smile. 'Nothing happened, but he boasted how good he'd been as a young man and she kidded him along. He said he was past it, but she told him he wasn't and he started giving her things.'

'Such as what?'

'Money. He also gave her a necklet – that one in the picture you had – and started talking about wanting her. She said she was a virgin and wasn't going to have any nonsense. She wasn't, of course, and what's a virgin, anyway? If you're not the first, someone else soon will be. But then he offered marriage. He said he'd been married before and started whining about being lonely and sick of having Mademoiselle Thing – what's her name? – Guichet – as the only woman in his life. Dominique said *she'd* marry him. It was a good idea, too. He was past it and was soon going to pop off, anyway.'

'So how did she come to be pregnant?'

Crussol gave a twisted grin. 'That was me. She was going to tell him it was his. He'd never have known. It was a super idea. He said he'd change his will in her favour. He'd only just made one, it seems, but he said he'd make another. He was a pushover. He was so old. He asked how old *she* was, so she asked him how old he'd like her to be. When he told her, that was the age she said she was. She was pretty clever. Up to all sorts of tricks.'

'Such as smuggling, for instance?'

Crussol's face fell. 'How did you find out about that?'

'Was it you who provided the brandy and got rid of the scotch?'

Crussol looked sick. 'It was nothing really.'

'I doubt if the magistrates would think so. Go on about Arne. What else happened?'

Crussol scowled. 'She disappeared, that's what. Some bastard got rid of her. Just when we were doing fine. You know what that old sock was worth? That damn' great house. All that land. All likely to go to a cat's home because he hadn't a relative in the world. He's got a quarry, too. The best stone you can get. I could have had all I wanted. When I hacked off toes, I could have just ordered a new block instead of trying to make a new foot and have it come out as if it were crippled. And space? I've always fancied doing something really big and there are rooms there thirty and forty feet high.'

'So why did you kill her?'

Crussol's jaw dropped. '*I* didn't kill her. Honest I didn't! Why should I? She could have kept me in stone for the rest of my life and I'd lick anybody's shoes for that. So why *would* I kill her? She was on her way to see me at Mongy when she disappeared. She must have been. She telephoned me. Here. She said she had something to tell me, but that she was telephoning from the house and had to be quick.'

'Why?'

'I don't know. She said she'd tell me when she saw me, so we arranged to meet.'

'What was it?'

'I don't know. And she never turned up so I never did find out. She said she'd found some old newspaper cuttings at Ivry. That's all I know.'

'Was she blackmailing someone? The old man?'

'She might have been. She'd tried it before. She said we had to get on with things so we arranged to meet in the bar opposite. I told you I was there. I was. All evening. But I didn't tell you why. *She* was why. When she didn't appear I decided she'd got cold feet. Or met some other guy. It would have been just like her to do something stupid like that.'

'What do you *think* it was she wanted to tell you?'

'I don't know. It sounded important. She asked me if I had a ring.'

'Why did she want a ring?'

'I think she had some idea of getting the marriage fixed up there and then. Perhaps she wanted me as a witness. Perhaps the old man was on his last legs and she wanted to make it legal before he popped off, so she could inherit everything.' Crussol sighed. 'She would have, too, you know, because he had no relations to object. None at all. He told her so. Name of God, with the kid that was coming, she *could* have pulled it off easy.' Crussol looked on the point of tears. 'She was certainly getting her value out of that kid. She made out it was Charnier's, too, and that poor bastard coughed up as well.'

'You knew him?'

'Oh, yes. I met him but he wasn't around much, and when he was around he wasn't much. The old man was the real prize. She was going to tell him that he had to make an honest woman of her. Then, after they were hitched, all we had to do was wait.'

'You might have had to wait a long time, my friend,' Pel said dryly. 'I was informed by Stocklin's doctor that he was good for another ten or fifteen years.'

Crussol's jaw dropped. 'That would have been just my luck,' he said. 'I expect she'd have bolted with the loot, anyway, and left me holding the can. But I didn't kill her. I swear I didn't.'

'Then if you didn't, who did?'

'I don't know. I wish I did. I'd strangle the bastard. He robbed me of the rest of my life. I could have had all the stone I wanted. Stone's expensive.'

'So I hear.' Pel indicated Jesus and Lazarus. 'So how did you pay for that? It's pretty big.'

Crussol frowned. 'Old Panique lifted one of the old boy's rings. He had a few things left over from his first wife and when he gave her that necklet she was wearing, she watched where he got it from. He made her turn her back but she was as crafty as he was and pretended to be putting on some lipstick so she could watch him through the mirror. He has a cupboard alongside his bed. He keeps whisky in it. Old Panique brought it in occasionally for him from Mongy. Underneath where the bottle stands there's a false bottom. You have to slide out a sort of shelf. The base looks solid but there's this little space. She took the ring out one day when they'd knocked him out with a sleeping pill and I sold it and bought the stone.'

Pel looked at Darcy. His head was pounding but the excitement of the case was making him feel better. 'What about Jo-Jo la Canne?' he asked.

'Who's he?'

'Did *you* kill him?'

'I've never even heard of him.' Crussol looked panic-stricken. 'I've been at work. Every day.'

'*He* was shot at night.'

'Well, it wasn't me. I don't go around shooting people. Besides, I've been putting in overtime. Working late. People have been dying a lot lately. They do, you know. It's a habit they have. I think there's a plague going round. Probably the Black Death. Another old bastard today somewhere. I told you.'

'Do you possess a gun?'

'What do I want a gun for?'

'Have you never had a gun?'

'No. Why?'

'Jo-Jo la Canne was killed by a gun.'

'Well, it wasn't me. I faint at the sight of blood. I – ' Crussol stopped dead, then his face changed ' – Dominique had a gun. At least she knew where one was kept.'

'Did she tell you?'

'Yes. It was the old man's. He kept it with the jewellery. Do you think old Panique shot this Jo-Jo type?'

'She'd been dead a long time when Jo-Jo was killed. I think you'd better come with us and make a statement.'

'Look – ' Crussol looked panic-stricken ' – I didn't kill her. Or this damned Jo-Jo!'

'No,' Darcy said. 'But, whatever the truth of that, you *were* involved in a conspiracy to defraud an old man.'

'Yes, well – that's different.'

'Not in the eyes of the law. You could go inside for it.'

'I can't! Not now! There's this stiff to box up. Some old guy they said had died suddenly.'

'I don't think he'll complain.'

Crussol became still. He had picked up the heavy stone hammer. 'You're arresting me?'

'We're asking you to come to headquarters and make a statement.'

'NO!' Suddenly Crussol's uncertain temper exploded. As he swung round, hurling the hammer, Pel ducked and the hammer hit the statue of Jesus raising Lazarus. A bottle followed, then anything Crussol could lay his hands on.

Darcy made a grab for him and went staggering back with a fist in his chest that felt like a trip hammer and Pel reeled away blinded by a glancing blow on the cheek. But as Crussol made a dive for the door, Bardolle swung. His fist was about the size of a bag of coal and it caught Crussol at the side of the head with a thump that sounded like the crack of doom. Crussol jerked upright, stiff and straight, then went down like a felled tree, bringing down with him a wooden manikin, the table holding the bottles and dirty glasses, a curtain and the curtain rail it hung from, a wooden screen and a pile of books and newspapers. As he fell to the floor, the curtain fell over him like a shroud.

They picked themselves up hurriedly, expecting another wild charge but, as Crussol threw off the curtain and rose, shedding books, newspapers and pieces of glass, his face fell as he saw where the hammer he'd thrown had landed.

'Look what you've made me do!' he wailed. 'You've made me break those damned toes again!'

twenty-two

Nosjean and Claudie Darel huddled over the table in the restaurant behind the Bar Transvaal. The dirty plates were piled to one side and the wine bottle contained nothing but dregs. Though Nosjean still kept slipping pieces of bread into his mouth, they had long since finished their meal but in their intense concentration on what they were saying they were totally unaware of the bored waiter watching them from the doorway.

For a fortnight, Nosjean, Claudie and De Troq' had been moving about between Paris and Lyons and between the Franco-German frontier and the Atlantic coast, making intensive enquiries. Though they had made progress it had been very, very slow.

'After Dole,' Nosjean was saying, 'our friend Sirdey seems to have moved to Paris where he made money selling insecticide. He bought it from a firm that went bust, packeted it in small containers with a bright label and sold it as an aid to gardening.'

'What about the woman he married?'

'Twenty-three. Monique Duat. She divorced him because he was never at home. Pretty. Same type as Josée Celine. She couldn't tell me much about him because she soon left him and he disappeared.'

'And then?' Claudie asked.

'She thought he went to the Bordeaux area. He seemed to like to put plenty of distance between himself and his last resting place.'

'Did he marry again?'

'I don't know yet. But there was a girl called Lefèvre in Royan who married a man called Bigéard who could be him because she was twenty-three again like Josée Celine and Monique Duat.'

'What happened to this one?'

'She was found dead in her bedroom, with Bigéard's gun alongside her. Properly licensed because he'd been dealing in precious stones, but he admitted he was having an affair with another woman. A verdict of suicide was recorded but there was so much ill-feeling for him in the town he decided to leave the district.'

'And then?'

'And then I don't know. But the girl he was having an affair with came from Aix-en-Provence so it's possible he moved there.'

'Have you found her?'

'No,' Nosjean admitted. 'She disappeared.'

'Dead? Murdered, like Josée Celine?'

'I've no idea yet. She wasn't from that area and nobody knew much about her. But *he* made more money and moved again.'

'Where to?'

Nosjean grinned. 'De Troq's enquiring,' he said. 'He's hard to keep up with.'

While Nosjean, Claudie and De Troq' struggled with their problem, Pel sat huddled in his chair doing his daily stint of reading the newspapers before going home. As usual they were all marked for his attention by Cadet Martin. There were the usual selection of murders, beatings-up and sexual attacks, even, he noticed, an attempt at rape by an 82-year-old man on a 55-year-old woman in a hotel in Amiens. Disgusted, he tossed the paper aside and sat for a moment in silence. His brain felt addled, his sinuses were painful, his eyes were red, watery and inflamed, and his head felt as if it were full of cotton wool. In addition, there was now a dark purple bruise on his cheek where Crussol's swinging fist had caught him.

The telephone rang. He snatched it up and was just about to snarl into it when he heard Madame Faivre-Perret's voice. His expression melted until he looked like a dog begging to be stroked.

'What are you doing at work?' she demanded. 'I gave you forty-eight hours, thinking you'd be in bed all the time but when I rang your home, Madame Routy said you hadn't been there at all except for a few hours' sleep.'

Pel cowered. It was the first sign of the iron fist beneath the velvet glove. 'There are things to be done,' he said. 'And I'm better. Nearly, anyway.'

He tried to explain that people who got themselves killed didn't wait for doses of flu in detectives to abate. She listened quietly and made him promise to go home early. Her concern pleased him enough to make him feel better.

'One day,' she said, 'I'll be there to look after you.'

Please God, Pel thought. As soon as possible.

Putting the telephone down, he sank back in his chair. The rings under his eyes made him look like a giant panda but the eyes themselves were bright and his brain was active. All the time his mind kept coming back to the fact that Jo-Jo la Canne had been shot, that old Stocklin had claimed to have a gun, and that Dominique Pigny had told Crussol where it was kept.

Had Crussol got hold of it somehow? Had Dominique Pigny? And if it *were* Crussol, why would he murder Dominique Pigny who was going to provide him with all the things he needed from old Stocklin's money? Or had he persuaded Jo-Jo la Canne to kill her and then somehow got hold of the gun to shoot Jo-Jo? Jo-Jo's death seemed to be explicable but not Dominique's, because she held the key to the crock of gold. And why would Stocklin have to alter his will if there were no relations? If there were no relations, why make one at all? And why had no one seen the white Mercedes sitting in the lay-by on the road from Arne to Mongy? It must have stuck out like a sore thumb. It just didn't make sense. It seemed important to go to Arne again.

Darcy was uneasy. He knew Philippe Duche was in the area somewhere, and he put on an operation that looked like a Para raid, with Bardolle's men everywhere.

'You make me feel stupid, Daniel,' Pel protested.

'You'd feel stupider if you stopped a bullet,' Darcy growled.

Driving up to the château, they were surprised to find the entrance covered with black draperies embroidered with silver tears.

'He's dead,' Guichet said as he let them in. 'Night before last.'

Pel looked about him at the drawn curtains. 'A bit unexpected, wasn't it?' he said. 'I thought he was good for a long time yet.'

Guichet shrugged. 'I think the doctor was taken by surprise. He was pretty old. Eighty-seven last May. Older than we thought. We found out as we went through his papers looking for his birth certificate.'

'What happened?' Pel asked. 'Heart?'

'Well, he didn't move very fast, and he liked his whisky. He also liked feather pillows. He seems to have drunk too much, turned over and smothered himself.'

Inside the house was a smell of flowers and candle-grease and there were candles burning in the hall.

'I'd like to see him,' Pel said.

The old man was lying in the coffin with candles burning at head and foot. Automatically, Pel took the sprig of rosemary from the bowl of holy water and made the sign of the cross over him.

Bernadine Guichet appeared, silently as a ghost. 'It was a bit sudden,' she said.

'Who found him?'

'I did.'

Pel stared at the dead man. His mouth was twisted in a rictus of a smile so that his waxen features had a look of cunning glee on them – as if he felt he'd defeated them all.

'I came in with his coffee and roll yesterday morning,' Mademoiselle Guichet said, 'and there he was. We called the doctor straight away. There was no argument. After all, Doctor Lecomte had been treating him for years. He issued a certificate at once. In this weather, you have to get on with it, so we contacted the undertakers at once.'

'Chevalliers'?' Pel asked. 'Of Châtillon?'

'Yes. How did you know?'

'Guessed,' Pel said, thinking of the irony of Gérard Crussol about to act as pallbearer to the man whose fortune he'd hoped to acquire.

'Were you fond of the old man?' he asked.

Mademoiselle Guichet shrugged. 'I suppose so,' she said. 'He was difficult, but he was old, and in my experience old people suffer a lot and don't complain. I think he'd fallen out of bed during the night. Doctor Lecomte found bruising on his shoulders. But he didn't ring and he didn't call out so he must have got back on his own. Perhaps he'd hurt himself and that's why he got out the whisky.'

'Who gets this place now?'

She shrugged. 'I don't know. I expect his lawyers will know. He said he'd left me a little for looking after him, but I don't know how much.'

Pel frowned. 'He told me he had a gun. He offered to shoot you, in fact.'

'He was always saying that. I think he was a rough man in his youth. He liked to boast about women – and about men he'd fought with.'

'Where did he keep it?'

'I often wished I knew. I don't suppose we'll ever find it now.'

Pet gestured at the cupboard alongside the bed, on top of which the old man had kept his glasses and his other belongings. 'What about in there?'

'It contained his whisky. That's all. I've just emptied it.'

'I'll still look.'

Watched by the Guichets, Pel opened the cupboard. It was an ugly piece of furniture that seemed to belong more in a Rhineland castle than in the middle of Burgundy and its lowest shelf seemed a solid square of mahogany. Tapping it, Pel began to feel towards the back. His fingers found a little niche and he broke a nail trying to pull it forward. Fishing a coin from his pocket, he inserted it in the niche and slowly, stiffly, the shelf slid towards him. Beneath it was a deep space that contained several faded jewel boxes. Taking them out one at a time, he opened them. Most of them contained jewellery, all of it old-fashioned and some of it ugly but all expensive-looking, though there was one gold bracelet that he recognised at once as another piece by Lucie and a ring with a huge diamond in it, which he studied for a moment before holding it up for Darcy to see. There was no gun.

As he looked up, he saw Mademoiselle Guichet's eyes on the jewellery. 'I think I'd better lock that up,' she said. 'It ought to go to the lawyers dealing with his estate.'

'For the time being we'll keep it. We'll give you a receipt.'

Still on his knees, Pel studied the space at the bottom of the cupboard, then he put the jewellery cases to his nose and sniffed. Watched by Darcy, he put his head in the cupboard and sniffed again. 'I can't smell a damn thing,' he said. 'I think I'm clogged up solid. You have a go, Daniel.'

'What am I smelling for, Patron?'

'Just sniff and tell me what you smell.'

Darcy lifted the jewellery cases to his nose, then he looked at Pel and, getting to his hands and knees, he put his head in the cupboard.

'What is it?' Guichet asked. 'Drugs?'

'No,' Darcy said. 'Gun oil. It has a smell all of its own. He kept a gun in there with the jewellery. Where is it now?'

Madame Guichet's shoulders lifted in a shrug.

'Have you ever seen the gun in there?'

'I've never seen in there at all. I didn't know it existed.'

On the way home, Darcy looked puzzled.

'Surely, Patron,' he said, 'you don't think the old man shot Jo-Jo?'

Pel gestured. Bells rang in his head and it felt as if the front was about to drop off and deposit his brains in his lap.

'There was a report in *France Soir* last night,' he said. 'About an attempted rape by an old man of eighty-two. If *he* had urges like that, perhaps Stocklin did too. Perhaps they were strong enough to make him insane with fury if he learned that Dominique Pigny only wanted him for his money. He might have got Jo-Jo to kill her.'

'But then he'd have to get rid of Jo-Jo, Patron.'

'He gets out of bed. We've seen him.'

'But could he also get out of the bedroom and out of the house, drive a car, meet Jo-Jo, shoot him, push him from the car, then climb out, cover him with leaves and hide the gun? Without being missed? Patron, it's not possible.'

Pel had to admit it didn't seem so.

Driven home in Aimedieu's car, Pel once more took the whisky bottle to bed with a hot water bottle. Madame Routy showed no interest in him at all. Considering he was clearly dying, he felt it showed a certain lack of good manners.

Snuffling and miserable, he huddled beneath the blankets but sleep refused to come. He had too much on his mind. Nothing seemed to make sense. Who had killed Dominique Pigny? If she were on the point of making a fortune out of the old man at Arne, surely, it couldn't have been Crussol. So was Jo-Jo la Canne somehow involved with her? And if so, why was he dead? And who'd killed him? Had the old man found out? He had a gun, but surely he couldn't have done it himself.

He finally fell into a fitful sleep with the questions still revolving round his brain. When he woke the following morning he decided he wasn't going to die after all, only linger on to a weak and feeble old age. Struggling into his clothes, he rejected Madame Routy's coffee. How she managed with the best beans available to make it taste like shellac he couldn't imagine.

Aimedieu appeared soon afterwards and, reaching his office and needing a cup of decent coffee, he rang his bell. It was Cadet Martin who answered it.

'Where's Claudie?' Pel demanded. He'd grown used to seeing Claudie's smile every morning and it irritated him to see Martin's anxious-rabbit look instead.

'She's up to something with Nosjean and De Troq', Patron. Nosjean's gone to Aix and De Troq' to Lyons.'

'I hope they'll be able to justify their expenses.'

For a while Pel sat staring at this blotter then, wearily, he put on his coat and hat again and, calling for Aimedieu, tottered off to the Bar Transvaal. Even though Aimedieu might not have to fend off assassins, he could always carry him back if he passed out. Catching sight of himself in the mirror above the bar, he thanked God Madame Faivre-Perret hadn't ever seen him at this hour of the morning.

A heavy hand slapped his shoulder. It was Darcy. He looked fit and well and in full possession of all his faculties. Pel hated him.

'How do you feel, Patron?' he said.

'I think I'm dying. Unless, of course, I'm dead already. I might well be.'

Darcy grinned, showing the white teeth he was so proud of. He looked as though he'd spent the night industriously and to his advantage.

'I hear Nosjean's on to a new scent,' he said.

'I wish I were. This whole thing is wrong. What was Dominique la Panique up to? Was she blackmailing Stocklin? Why otherwise collect press cuttings from Concarneau and Lyons? What had she found out? And what's the connection with Josée Celine who was dead before she was born? There must have been some to make her ask questions at the caves. And why did old Stocklin make a will when he had no relations? It's something we need to find out.'

None of the local lawyers had handled Stocklin's business but, because of the size of his property, it occurred to Pel that one of the estate agents might know something. One did and gave them the name of a lawyer in Auxerre who had handled the purchase.

Cadet Martin found the number of the lawyer and Pel spoke for a long time. As he listened, he sat up sharply then, for the next hour, holding a handkerchief to his nose while Cadet Martin alternately brought him cups of strong black coffee to keep him awake, and bottles of cold beer from the Bar Transvaal to slake the thirst caused by his fever, he crouched over the instrument.

His office grew stuffy enough for Martin to gasp for breath as he appeared but Pel remained on the telephone. First to Concarneau, then to Lyons. He seemed to be tracing old people, talking to newspapers and to police. It went on until midday and when Cadet Martin went for lunch, the man on the switchboard turned round. 'What's happening up there?' he asked. 'Has war been declared? The Old Man's making enough telephone calls for a general mobilisation.'

At three o'clock, Pel decided he'd had enough and, calling for Aimedieu, had himself driven home. Madame Routy took one look at him and turned down the volume of the television. Despite his headache, it made Pel feel better. He was finally winning the war against her.

He was unable to sleep because his mind was too busy and he spent the time tossing and turning underneath the blankets like a wounded whale. About eleven o'clock, the telephone went. It was Brochard, who was doing telephone duty at the Hôtel de Police.

'I've got a message for you, Patron,' he said. 'I'm sorry it's so late. It was a type called Le Bihan. He said you'd want to know at once. He said he's found out about that old woman you were asking about. He just said "Tell him that the family house was used as an old people's home." Does it make sense to you?'

'Yes,' Pel said. 'It does. I think I'll be able to sleep now.'

twenty-three

Pel wasn't the only man receiving late night telephone calls. Nosjean received one, too. He lived with his parents and three adoring unmarried sisters who loved to accept messages which they felt took their brother into all the corridors of espionage, top secrecy and crime.

'It's for you.' Nosjean, fast asleep on the settee, supposedly watching the late night film on television, sat up sharply.

'Who is it?'

'He said his name was De Troq'. Is he that baron you know?'

'Yes.'

'Is he a secret service man?'

Nosjean grinned. 'He's a cop. Like me.'

De Troq's voice was excited. 'I've found him!' he yelled. 'He's our man! And what's more I know where he went to from here.'

'Where?'

De Troq' told him and Nosjean grinned. 'Something to celebrate,' he said.

'I've already celebrated.'

'I thought you had,' Nosjean said. 'Make sure you're here first thing in the morning. We'll need to catch the Old Man.'

Unfortunately the Old Man arrived before they were ready. He looked like death because, despite what he'd said, he hadn't been able to sleep after all; but, because he hadn't been able to sleep, he'd been doing a lot of thinking and there was an aggressive glint in his eyes. Darcy arrived shortly afterwards, brisk and businesslike.

'I've laid on Aimedieu and Brochard,' he said. 'And I've telephoned Bardolle.'

'That'll be enough,' Pel said. 'We don't need a division of tanks.'

They climbed into Darcy's car and they had no sooner disappeared from sight when Nosjean arrived. He entered the building looking tired but pleased with himself. Under his arm was a thick file of documents. Cadet Martin was in the office going through the newspapers like a propaganda minister on the look-out for slip-ups.

'Where's the Chief?' Nosjean asked.

'He's out.'

'Where?'

Martin told him and as Nosjean headed at speed back for the sergeants' room, De Troq' appeared with Claudie Darel.

'He's out,' Nosjean said. 'I think we ought to contact him.'

They ran down the stairs, deciding to take De Troq's car because it was bigger and faster than Nosjean's. Piling in, they shot from the car park as if they were coming out from the start at Le Mans.

The churchyard was a bleak little patch surrounded by a high wall, the grass between the tombs brown and withered after the sun. The smell of dead flowers seemed to pervade the place as Pel, Darcy and the other two detectives took up a position under the trees where they couldn't be seen.

A few black-clad people whom they recognised from Arne were standing near the open grave, sheepish-looking as if they'd been paid to attend – the Guichets, the man from the village café, the young man who drove the tractor at the farm, his heavy hands screwing at his cap. The sun was warm and the place was silent, not a breath of wind stirring the trees.

'It's peaceful, isn't it?' Brochard said.

'You'd hardly expect it to be a riot,' Darcy snapped. 'And you're not here to admire the place, you're here to keep your eyes open for men with guns.'

When the priest's muttering had finished, the few mourners moved round the grave, tossing handfuls of earth into the hole from a spade held out to them by the grave-digger, then they crossed themselves and headed for the exit. There were only two cars, the station wagon from the château which had brought the Guichets, and a shabby old Renault into which the rest of the mourners crammed.

As they disappeared, Pel jerked his head and they headed towards their car. They had just left when De Troquereau's big roadster hurtled round the corner and slid to a stop in the dust. There appeared to be no sign of their quarry. Then Claudie's hand jerked out.

'There,' she said, pointing. 'Going up the hill there! That's Darcy's car!'

They were just leaving the village when Darcy frowned.

'There's some damned lunatic behind us flashing his lights,' he said. 'I've a good mind to run him in for dangerous driving. He's – Mother of God, it's that damned liner of De Troq's! What the hell does *he* want? He's got Nosjean in the front with him.'

Pel turned. 'And Claudie in the rear. Pull over, Daniel.'

As Darcy pulled into the grass verge, De Troq's car swung in front of it and came to a stop. The doors flew open and Nosjean, De Troq' and Claudie Darel fell out.

Pel stepped from Darcy's car. 'What in the name of God's going on?' he said.

'We have to talk to you, Patron,' Nosjean said.

'Not now!'

Nosjean glanced at De Troq' and drew a deep breath. 'Patron – '

'NOT NOW!'

'We've got something for you.'

Pel glared. 'Not now, I said. I've got enough on at the moment and I feel like death, anyway.'

Nosjean drew a deep breath. 'Patron,' he said loudly, 'there's something you should know.'

'I don't want to know anything.'

'It's about Josée Celine.'

'That's *your* case.'

'No, Patron,' Nosjean said firmly. 'I think it's become *yours*.'

There was a long silence. Pel stared at Nosjean, then he blew his nose heavily. Nosjean, De Troq' and Claudie stood in front of him like the accused at a murder trial. Darcy watched, puzzled.

'Inform me,' Pel said.

Nosjean fished inside De Troq's car for the folder he'd brought. 'It's all here, Patron,' he said. 'Every last bit of it.'

Pel frowned. 'I'm not in the habit of reading reports or holding conferences in the middle of the highway,' he growled.

'There's a café about a kilometre further on, Patron,' Nosjean urged. 'Perhaps we could go there.'

'I'm also not in the habit of dealing with police business in public places.'

'Patron,' Nosjean said earnestly. 'It's *important*. They have a back room. I'm sure they'd lend it to us.'

Without a word, Pel climbed back into Darcy's car and allowed Nosjean to lead the way. The café smelled of stale wine but there were two rooms and the proprietor agreed to close the door of one of them. They sat down round a table stained with the rings from wine glasses and beer mugs and began to light cigarettes. Eventually the proprietor arrived with two bottles of wine.

Pel waited without speaking until the wine had been poured and the door closed. Then he gestured at Nosjean's file.

'Inform me,' he said.

Watched by the others, Nosjean opened the file and began to spread papers across the table. 'I told you it would be difficult, Patron,' he said, 'because Sirdey covered his tracks so well. But he *did* join the Milice – we established that – and he did work with the Nazis for a while. He was even wanted by the Resistance down near Vercors. He also made money through the Black Market and when the war ended he disappeared. That was where it became difficult.'

Nosjean paused, moving the papers with his hands. Pel listened quietly, his face impassive, holding a handkerchief to his nose.

'But then it suddenly took off,' Nosjean said. 'And when it did, it went like wildfire. I knew it would. After covering his tracks for twenty years, he finally decided he was safe and grew less careful. Paris turned him up for us. They had a photograph, which we didn't have because all ours were destroyed by a bomb during the war. It seemed to match the one we'd picked up which is a pretty indifferent one taken from the newspaper files. Photography, like a lot of other things, was difficult at the time because all photographic material was directed towards the Germans, and the newspapers didn't publish any pictures.'

He gestured at a photograph on the table. It showed a tall, heavily bearded man wearing thick dark-rimmed spectacles.

'It *seemed* like our man,' Nosjean went on. 'But it could just as easily have been Yves Montand with a false beard. But we did a bit of checking and finally we decided it *was* him. He'd started a business buying surplus war material. After that, though, there were no photographs because he'd started being very careful. We traced him to Royan but he didn't stay there long. He'd had three or four wives we knew about but he was over fifty by this time, Patron, so he must have had a way with him. He went to Nantes.'

'And then?'

'And then we lost him, Patron.' Nosjean smiled. 'But now we've got the lot. I went to Aix and De Troq' took on Lyons. We tied it up. We've got the whole history.'

Pel said nothing, merely waving to Nosjean to explain.

Nosjean showed him the file. 'It's all here, Patron. Every bit of it. Xavier Sirdey married a girl called Léonie Gensoul, aged twenty-three, in Toulouse in 1933. For a man who seems to have liked women, he was pretty old – already thirty-five – so he'd probably married another girl – perhaps two – before then. The next thing we know is that he went through a form of marriage with Josée Celine, née Joséphine Cellino, in 1942, when he was already married to Léonie Gensoul. She disappeared and we then find him first in Dole as Georges Morot, then as Oscar Ferry and married now to Henriette Devoise, again 23, also in Dole. Then he disappears and turns up, again in Paris, still as Oscar Ferry, married to Monique Duat, daughter of a wealthy lawyer.'

'He's another Landru, this one.'

'Yes, Patron, and I think he certainly did away with more than one of his wives. After Monique Duat, he changed his name to Jean-Jacques Bigéard and married Marianne Lefèvre, twenty-three again, in Royan. He was growing pretty wealthy by this time and went into property. It wasn't long after the war and bombing had caused a lot of damage in Royan. He built several houses and bungalows at St. Georges-de-Didonne nearby, and acquired an interest in a cement firm which was very useful because most of Royan, including the church, was rebuilt with concrete. He was making a lot of money there when his wife was found dead with his gun alongside her. He admitted having an affair with another girl, Michelline Auriac, of Aix – '

'Aged twenty-three?'

'Yes, Patron. A verdict of suicide was recorded, but there was so much ill-feeling he left the district with the Auriac girl. By this time he was around sixty. But he hadn't finished yet because we next find him married to her. He's more than likely a bigamist two or three times over because we've only come up with one divorce. Nothing further is known of Michelline Auriac. She's believed to have moved towards Mulhouse but it's been impossible to confirm.'

'Could he have killed her, too?' Darcy asked.

'We were in touch with Aix.' Nosjean tossed another sheet of paper to the table. 'They had their suspicions. They sent a photograph of Michelline Auriac and said they'd be grateful for any information we could supply. Finally – ' more sheets floated to the table ' – under the name of Robert Sergeant he went through a form of marriage with Catherine Delorme, of Lyons, who left him when she discovered he was still married to Michelline Auriac and – if *she* was dead which we believe – to Marianne Lefèvre as well. Catherine Delorme was also twenty-three.'

'There seems to be something magic about that age,' Pel said. 'You have seven you know about and two probables.'

'Yes, Patron. But finally De Troq' heard in Lyons that he's moved north.'

'Back to his home ground? Would he do that?'

'My Indian Runners did,' De Troq' said.

Pel was silent for a moment. 'And me?' he asked. 'Where do I come into this?'

Silently, Nosjean reached across and laid a photograph of Léonie Gensoul on the table in front of him. 'She's the wife in Toulouse,' he said. 'She's one of those who disappeared, probably dead.'

Pel picked up the photograph and studied it closely. Then he looked up slowly. 'She's wearing the same necklet Dominique Pigny was wearing,' he said.

There was a long silence, then Pel picked up another photograph.

'Josée Celine,' Nosjean said. 'She's also wearing the necklet. Claudie went to see Madame Frémion again. She has a lot of photographs of Josée Celine. The ones she originally picked out for us were all stage portraits and publicity pictures and were all taken before she met Sirdey. She wasn't wearing the necklet in any of them so nothing clicked. But when Claudie asked to see *all* her photos, she found several like this.'

Nosjean shuffled them out like a pack of cards. 'She's wearing the necklet in every one of them,' he said. 'And *these* were taken *after* she met Sirdey. In that one – ' his finger jabbed ' – she's also wearing the diamond ring and the earrings he gave her. Madame Frémion said they were family heirlooms so perhaps *all* his women wore them at one time or another. But he knew their value and made sure he got them back when he finished with them. He not only removed the necklet from Josée's neck, he also removed the ring from her finger and the earrings from her ears.'

Pel remained silent and Nosjean went on. 'Sirdey would be around eight-five or six now. He was born in 1896, the second son to the third wife of Alphonse Sirdey, of Nevers. His father, who died in 1916, was born in 1821. 1821, Patron!' Nosjean sounded awed. 'Which means, Patron, that he was ninety-five when he died and seventy-five when he sired Xavier Sirdey. They're long livers.'

'They're also long fornicators,' Darcy said bluntly. He looked at Pel. 'Patron, that old bastard at Arne – what Crussol said makes sense. Perhaps he *did* get the girl in his bed. Perhaps even they had some fun and games. If his father could, perhaps he could, too.'

Pel was deep in thought as Nosjean placed his file in front of him.

'Yours, I'm afraid, Patron,' he said. 'Everything on Xavier Sirdey, alias Georges Morot, alias Oscar Ferry, alias Jean-Jacques Bigéard, alias Robert Sergeant. I've seen the photographs of the bullet that killed Jo-Jo la Canne and the photographs of the one that killed Michelline Auriac. Whether she died by accident or design, she was killed by the same gun. A MAS 6.35. The only thing that doesn't fit snugly into it all is that Dominique Pigny was thirty-one.'

Pel looked up. 'That,' he said, 'is because she was careful to ask him what age he preferred and when he told her, that was what she decided to be. It must have been twenty-three.'

Nosjean nodded. 'Your Stocklin, Patron,' he said, 'is our Sirdey.'

twenty-four

'Three murders,' Nosjean said, still excited with their success. 'Possibly four.'

Pel finished his wine. 'More than that,' he said mildly. 'Probably two or three others you don't know about.'

'Hadn't we better get up there then, Patron, and haul him in?'

'I don't think he'll run away,' Pel said. 'He's dead. He was buried this afternoon. We've just watched him put down.'

Nosjean's jaw dropped and he glanced at De Troq' and Claudie. They looked like stockbrokers who'd had a bad day.

'Don't worry,' Pel said, 'your journey won't be wasted.' He reached into his brief case and started to lay his own documents on the table.

'Jacqueline Cochet,' he said. 'Nurse. Thirty-nine years old. Alias Jacqueline Poupon. Alias Bernadine Guichet. Two years ago she visited the Château d'Ivry, knowing it to be owned by an old part-bedridden man. I got her name and description from the lawyer in Auxerre who had handled the sale of the property to Sirdey-Stocklin-or-whatever-you-like-to-call-him. She'd found out about the sale and she was wondering if there would be a chance in the near future of the property changing hands again because she was interested. She was on the look-out for a rest home she could use for old people, which was something she knew about because when her mother died in Concarneau in circumstances which, it seems, were somewhat dubious, she used her house for that purpose.'

Pel sniffed and dabbed at his nose with his handkerchief. 'She later tried to get a loan from the bank to start another bigger home with another house in Lyons,' he went on. 'The bank turned her down but, by a strange coincidence, the owner of the house, one Raoul Zeller, who was an old man in his terminal illness, nursed by a woman called Jacqueline Poupon, died very soon afterwards. "Natural causes" was given as the reason but, in view of what I've told them, the police in Lyons are seeking an exhumation order and there's more than a chance that they'll find arsenic, because not only does Jacqueline Poupon bear a marked resemblance to Jacqueline Cochet but someone who answers to the description of Hubert Guichet found a job with Zeller as a gardener just before his death and was engaged in killing rats that were nesting under the garage.'

Pel paused. 'After Zeller's death,' he went on, 'Mademoiselle Cochet, alias Poupon, alias Guichet, inherited the house and did well enough to think of expanding yet again. Then she heard of the Château d'Ivry. Stocklin had just frightened his last housekeeper out of the house and was considering moving, but instead he took a fancy to her because she isn't bad-looking. So she began to think she might even get the place for nothing because she had a way with men, which is not surprising because it seems she once worked as a prostitute in Marseilles, where she still has three children in a children's home. Instead of continuing her efforts to buy the property, she took a job with Stocklin as his housekeeper and so on afterwards established Hubert Guichet as her assistant. She was beginning to do very well with Stocklin by this time and he had even made a will in her favour when Dominique Pigny arrived on the scene. And Dominique Pigny was younger than she was, had a better figure and even claimed to be twenty-three – which, as you've discovered, seems to have been a sort of talisman to Stocklin or Sirdey or whatever you wish to call him – and an age and shape Bernadine Guichet most manifestly was not. In Dominique Pigny also, Bernadine Guichet – née Cochet – came up against someone as clever as she was. Her nose was pushed out and something had to be done.

'Hubert Guichet – who has a record and is not her brother but her husband – knew Jo-Jo la Canne from their days in Marseilles. By this time, Dominique Pigny had discovered what the Guichets were up to. She'd recognised them from reports which had appeared in the newspapers at the time of the death of Jacqueline Cochet's mother. Dominique Pigny had lived around Concarneau as a teenager, you'll remember, and doubtless read of it in the papers when it happened. When she saw the Guichets she doubtless remembered and took a trip to Concarneau to look up the newspaper files. When she found out what she wanted to know, she went to Lyons and learned what they'd been up to there. Now she only had to warn Stocklin and they'd have been out on their ears. She could even have made it more permanent by informing the police. I don't think this is what she was going to tell Crussol but I believe the Guichets *thought* it was.

'As it happened, she had other better irons in the fire which she had to attend to first. She was out to get Sirdey's name on a will leaving everything to her. She was probably even hoping to blackmail him into it because he must have let something drop at some point about the cave at Drax and she'd been to Drax and paid her three francs fifty to get in. But nobody knew anything and she was in the wrong cave, anyway, so she found nothing. But that didn't stop her making guesses. And her guesses told her what you've just found out as fact. She probably also made a few enquiries around the newspaper offices and came to the conclusion that Stocklin was Sirdey. Perhaps she found photographs.

Or papers. I don't know, but she was determined to get her hands on his money and, having got it, as his wife she could blackmail him to her heart's content to let her spend it.

'She didn't consider the Guichets a problem because she had something on them, too. But, if they didn't know what she'd got on Stocklin, they must have guessed what she'd got on *them* and when she telephoned Crussol they heard her and that's what they thought she was talking about. They arranged for Jo-Jo to remove her. He stole the Mercedes and waited. The Guichets were watching from Stocklin's room and doubtless tipped him off to her identity with some sort of signal from a window as she left – a flapping towel or something of that sort. Jo-Jo ran her down, pushed her into the boot and drove through the night to Concarneau.'

The room was silent as everybody hung on Pel's words as they had on Nosjean's.

'By this time,' he went on, 'the Guichets were growing worried because *we'd* started asking questions. When we produced pictures of La Panique, the old man appeared to have lost his spectacles and couldn't identify her. But, you'll remember, Daniel, Mademoiselle Guichet went to his room first to make sure he was awake and I expect she removed them. Having got rid of Dominique, the Guichets were prepared to wait for old Stocklin to die, only to have Dr Lecomte inform them that he was likely to live to be a hundred. That was a long time to wait and they liked quick results. They wanted Stocklin's money, but they also now had to get rid of Jo-Jo who was obviously going to be dangerous. So one of them – Hubert, I expect – shot him with Stocklin's gun. They said they didn't know it existed, but I think they did. It didn't take Dominique long to spot the hiding place and they'd been in the house longer than she had.'

'They hadn't touched the jewellery, Patron,' Darcy said.

Pel sniffed, blew his nose and shrugged. 'They didn't have to,' he pointed out. 'According to Stocklin's will – the one he didn't have time to alter – the house and its contents were theirs for the taking. All they had to do was exactly what they proceeded to do – get rid of Stocklin.'

twenty-five

As Pel stopped talking, there was a long silence. For a moment nobody moved, then De Troq' shifted restlessly in his seat and Nosjean scraped back his chair.

Pel looked at his watch. 'I think perhaps we'd better be on our way,' he said quietly.

As he rose, Darcy pushed him back into his chair. 'I'll go ahead,' he said. 'Duche's probably prowling about out there Give me ten minutes.'

Pel frowned. 'I'm growing a little tired of this tomfoolery, Daniel.'

Darcy was unrepentant. 'I'm not, Patron. You'd better have another drink. See that he does, Claudie.'

Heading up the hill, he found Bardolle in the woods near the entrance to the château. He looked worried.

'There's somebody creeping about up there,' he said, gesturing at the slopes.

They climbed the hill, Bardolle surprisingly quick considering his bulk. As they reached the brow, working along the fence by the line of trees, Bardolle gestured.

'There he is!' he said.

In the valley, moving towards the road, they could see a man in a khaki shirt and trousers wearing a dark, square-shaped cap.

'It's a cop,' Darcy said.

'It's not one of my men,' Bardolle growled. 'I told them to stay up high where they could see.'

As they hurried down the slope, they heard cars arriving at the château. As they swung in to the drive and halted outside the door, Darcy began to push forward at greater speed.

At the great front door, still draped with its silver-decorated black draperies, the party paused. As Nosjean pushed it open and they stepped inside, Guichet appeared from his sitting room. He was holding a glass in his hand.

'Champagne?' Pel's voice was at its silkiest. 'Are you celebrating something?'

At his words, Bernadine Guichet appeared, also holding a glass. She was quicker to recover than her husband.

'Stocklin,' she said. 'It's a relief for him.'

'I wouldn't have thought it an occasion for champagne, all the same. Unless, of course, he left you something in his will. Did he?'

She glanced at her husband. 'Well, yes,' she said. 'A little.'

'How much?'

'As a matter of fact, he left it all to me.'

'I thought he might have. What a pity you won't be able to enjoy it.'

She frowned. 'What do you mean?'

'I'm afraid I'm going to ask you to accompany us to the city. There are a few questions I wish to ask you. About the death of your mother, Madame Cochet, of Concarneau, and about the death of a certain Raoul Zeller, of Lyons.'

She went pale.

'Finally,' Pel ended, 'about the death of one Charles-Louis Stocklin, once known, it seems, as Xavier Sirdey and numerous other names.'

'He died in his bed!'

'I expect the Forensic Lab and those bruises on his shoulders will show how.'

The Guichets stared at them, their faces as blank as brick walls, then, suddenly, Hubert Guichet dived for the door.

As he leapt past, Nosjean stuck out his foot and he went down, to slide on his front along the polished floor, taking with him the rug and a three-legged mahogany stand holding a plant. As he struggled among the scattered earth to rise, De Troq' wrenched his hands behind him and clapped on the handcuffs.

Claudie moved towards his wife, whose face went red.

'You bastards,' she spat.

As the party appeared in the doorway, Darcy was drawing nearer his quarry. He could see Duche clearly now through the bushes. He looked haggard and dirty as if he'd been sleeping rough, but his elbows were resting on the low branch of a tree, the rifle pointing towards the château for a perfect, unimpeded shot. So much for Pel's contempt, he thought.

He was afraid he was going to be too late and Duche heard the frantic crashing of the undergrowth and turned. As Darcy broke free he swung with the rifle barrel. Darcy ducked but it caught him a glancing blow on the side of the head to send him flying into the bushes. But Bardolle was just behind him, his big bulk smashing through the trees, and as Duche turned to meet him, he kicked his feet from under him then, as he scrambled to his knees, clasped his great hands together and brought them down together on the back of Duche's head. The rifle dropped and Duche took a nose dive into the grass, his face buried in the turned earth. Bardolle dusted his trousers carefully, took out his handcuffs and, whipping Duche's hands up, clamped them together behind his back.

Pel listened carefully as Darcy explained.

'I'm glad it's over,' he said quietly. 'And thank you, Daniel, for taking care of it. I'll make a point of seeing Bardolle and thanking him, too.'

'He's useful, that one,' Darcy said, his eyes still rolling from the crack on the head. 'He thinks a lot and moves fast when he has to.'

As they gathered by the cars, the two Guichets sitting stiff-backed alongside the dazed Philippe Duche, Pel sniffled and blew his nose. He'd decided he didn't like working on cases involving old people. They reminded him too much of how life shot by, and now that the excitement had died he was feeling terrible again.

'We seem to have turned up something big, Patron,' Darcy said.

'Bigger than we thought,' Pel agreed. 'But it seems that in the end everybody's got their come-uppance. Dominique got hers. Jo-Jo got his. The Guichets got theirs.'

'And Sirdey finally got his.'

Pel nodded. 'Poetic justice, wouldn't you say?' He was looking placidly self-satisfied. 'Payment deferred. Their punishment was slow coming but it came.'

He paused to stare about him. 'This lot – ' he was feeling wise and philosophical ' – predators, all four. But they all dodged the punishment for their crimes for years until suddenly – because they all came together – it caught up with them.' He held up his fist with the thumb extended. 'One: Jo-Jo la Canne. Known – though never proved – to have killed Tony the Tout and Marie Topin.' He lifted his first finger. 'Xavier Sirdey, alias Charles-Louis Stocklin, Oscar Ferry and a few other things. During the war a traitor working for the enemy. Known to have killed Josée Celine and probably Léonie Gensoul, Marianne Lefèvre, Michelline Auriac and probably a few French patriots besides.' Another finger rose. 'Three: Jacqueline Cochet, also known as Bernadine Guichet – and her husband. Believed to have killed her mother and Raoul Zeller for their property – to say nothing of Xavier Sirdey.' A third finger lifted. 'Four: Along comes Dominique Pigny. Another predator. Drifter and drop-out, possessing a record for theft and fraud and planning more of it here. But – ' Pel paused ' – she was the catalyst that destroyed them all. Because of her, they've all cancelled each other out. She was instrumental in bringing to an end all their evils and they hers.' He paused then lifted the last finger, the little finger. 'Even – since she brought me here and I brought Philippe Duche – him, too. Five of them. What a pity it can't happen more often. It would save us all a lot of trouble. There seems to be a touch of God's mercy about it.'

He drew a deep breath then climbed into the car and sat down tiredly, a bone at a time. But there was a look of satisfaction on his face.

'And now,' he said, 'I think you can look after things, Daniel, and if she doesn't mind taking a chance on catching something that's likely to be as deadly as the Black Death, I'll have Claudie drive me home. I'm going to bed. Perhaps you'll inform Madame Faivre-Perret that I've managed it at last.'

Mark Hebden

Death Set to Music

The severely battered body of a murder victim turns up in provincial France and the sharp-tongued Chief Inspector Pel must use all his Gallic guile to understand the pile of clues building up around him, until a further murder and one small boy make the elusive truth all too apparent.

The Errant Knights

Hector and Hetty Bartlelott go to Spain for a holiday, along with their nephew Alec and his wife Sibley. All is well under a Spanish sun until Hetty befriends a Spanish boy on the run from the police and passionate Spanish Anarchists. What follows is a hard-and-fast race across Spain, hot-tailed by the police and the anarchists, some light indulging in the Semana Santa festivities of Seville to throw off the pursuers, and a near miss in Toledo where the young Spanish fugitive is almost caught.

Mark Hebden

Pel and the Bombers

When five murders disturb his sleepy Burgundian city on Bastille night, Chief Inspector Evariste Clovis Désiré Pel has his work cut out for him. A terrorist group is at work and the President is due shortly on a State visit. Pel's problems with his tyrannical landlady must be put aside while he catches the criminals.

"...downbeat humour and some delightful dialogue."
Financial Times

Pel and the Paris Mob

In his beloved Burgundy, Chief Inspector Pel finds himself incensed by interference from Paris, but it isn't the flocking descent of rival policemen that makes Pel's blood boil – crimes are being committed by violent gangs from Paris and Marseilles. Pel unravels the riddle of the robbery on the road to Dijon airport as well as the mysterious shootings in an iron foundry. If that weren't enough, the Chief Inspector must deal with the misadventures of the delightfully handsome Sergeant Misset and his red-haired lover.

"...written with downbeat humour and some delightful dialogue which leaven the violence." *Financial Times*

Mark Hebden

Pel Under Pressure

The irascible Chief Inspector Pel is hot on the trail of a crime syndicate in this fast-paced, gritty crime novel, following leads on the mysterious death of a student and the discovery of a corpse in the boot of a car. Pel uncovers a drug-smuggling ring within the walls of Burgundy's university, and more murders guide the Chief Inspector to Innsbruck where the mistress of a professor awaits him.

Portrait in a Dusty Frame

The sudden popularity of the poet, Christina Moray Tait, seventy years after her death, gives her great-grandson, Tennyson Moray Tait, a new-found notoriety. When approached by a man claiming he could reveal the true circumstances surrounding Christina's mysterious death, Tennyson decides to join him in Peru, facing the dark green extremes of the Amazon, a reluctant American freelance photographer, and a suspicious native guide.

TITLES BY MARK HEBDEN AVAILABLE DIRECT FROM HOUSE OF STRATUS

Quantity		£	$(US)	$(CAN)	€
☐	The Dark Side of the Island	6.99	11.50	15.99	11.50
☐	Death Set to Music	6.99	11.50	15.99	11.50
☐	The Errant Knights	6.99	11.50	15.99	11.50
☐	Eye Witness	6.99	11.50	15.99	11.50
☐	A Killer for the Chairman	6.99	11.50	15.99	11.50
☐	League of Eighty Nine	6.99	11.50	15.99	11.50
☐	Mask of Violence	6.99	11.50	15.99	11.50
☐	Pel Among the Pueblos	6.99	11.50	15.99	11.50
☐	Pel and the Touch of Pitch	6.99	11.50	15.99	11.50
☐	Pel and the Bombers	6.99	11.50	15.99	11.50
☐	Pel and the Faceless Corpse	6.99	11.50	15.99	11.50
☐	Pel and the Missing Persons	6.99	11.50	15.99	11.50
☐	Pel and the Paris Mob	6.99	11.50	15.99	11.50
☐	Pel and the Party Spirit	6.99	11.50	15.99	11.50

ALL HOUSE OF STRATUS BOOKS ARE AVAILABLE FROM GOOD BOOKSHOPS OR DIRECT FROM THE PUBLISHER:

Internet: www.houseofstratus.com including author interviews, reviews, features.

Email: sales@houseofstratus.com please quote author, title and credit card details.